Greater Love Hath No Man

Charles Dale & Ross Wood

CEDAR HILL PUBLISHING

Greater Love Hath No Man

Copyright © 2004 Charles Dale & Ross Wood All Rights Reserved

No part of this publication may be reproduced, stored in a retrieval system, or transmitted in any form or by any means, electronic, mechanical, photocopying, recording or otherwise, without the prior written permission of the copyright owner.

Cover art by Kasie D. Shaw

Cover design by Rebecca Hayes

Preliminary edit by Tara Lang Chapman

Book design and editing by Rebecca Hayes

Published in the United States by
Cedar Hill Publishing
P.O. Box 905
Snowflake, Arizona 85937

Library of Congress Control Number: 2004109841

ISBN 1-932373-80-2

"For God shall bring every work into judgment, with every secret thing, whether it be good, or whether it be evil."

~Ecclesiastes 12:14

Coming Soon!

Part II:
A Day Like Today

Look for it in 2005!

Visit the Author's website for more information on this and forthcoming books and events!

http://www.charlesdale.info

Greater Love Hath No Man

Chapter one

Snow mixed with rain as it blew across a small Virginia town in March of 1863. A silver-gray mare, camouflaged by the winter surroundings, stood high on a ridge. A six- foot, five-inch tall man named Henry Watkins sloshed his way through the muddy snow toward the horse. Speaking quietly to the animal, he continued to step closer, until he reached the horse.

As he reached for the saddle horn, he whispered, "Easy girl; easy now." She stood quietly, allowing her master to mount her. Once seated in the saddle, Henry carefully guided his horse down the slope toward a trail. The trail intersected the only road that went to the well-traveled pike.

Greater Love Hath No Man

As he neared the pike, gunshots rang out nearby. Dismounting, he crept slowly up a small knoll that overlooked a hollow. He carefully peered over the top and saw several Federal soldiers shooting at a band of Confederates who had taken cover behind fallen trees. Henry watched as the Federals successfully used their sixteen-shot repeaters against shotguns, pistols and a few old breechloader flintlocks.

It was obvious who was winning this fight. The only thing at which the Rebels prevailed was name-calling as they cursed the Federals with all the profanity they could muster.

From this position, Henry could see the battle from above, and the soldiers on both sides were clearly visible. He saw a wounded Federal officer and knew this would soon be over if he didn't get involved. He slowly raised his rifle and aimed as the words "thou shalt not kill" echoed through his mind. His rifle fired, and a canteen lying close to the hit officer flew into the air.

The Federals didn't know where the shot had originated or who had fired it. They assumed they were out-maneuvered and began to retreat as the Rebels, thinking they had reinforcements, charged the Federals with yells and hoots of victory.

"Who the hell was up on that ridge?" yelled one of the Rebel soldiers.

Another answered, "I don't know, but he can't shoot worth a damn!" Little did they know that their benefactor had won every shooting contest that his county presented.

The last words of one of their dying comrades were, "You fellows don't know a gift from God when you see it."

Henry slowly eased from the knoll and returned to his horse. As he mounted the animal, he thought, *should I give this a few more minutes?* He listened for the sound of anyone approaching. Hearing nothing, he eased his horse back onto the trail. It was certain he wouldn't travel the pike now. He knew every obscure trail that ran parallel. His problem was that the Federals knew them, too.

As Henry rode, his thoughts drifted to the past and to his grandfather who had served with General Washington when they defeated the Hessians. Henry remembered the story his grandfather often told about being with Washington in the boat that crossed the Delaware. When people would ask Henry's grandfather if Washington really threw a dollar across the river, he would chuckle and say, "If he had and I had known it, I'da gone after it." This story and a section of land had been handed down through two generations and it was Henry's purpose to see that it stayed that way. It was this, in fact, which had him out traveling that day.

Cries from political leaders concerning statehood were coming out of Independence Hall in Wheeling. His neighbors and himself had voted for the existence of West Virginia, but rumors about the union confiscating farms from southern patriots began to worry him.

His father had been killed at a place called Buena Vista, Mexico while serving his country under the leadership of "old rough and ready Taylor." He left his two sons to help their mother manage things. The following year brought more hardship when pneumonia took Henry's mother's life, leaving seventeen-year-old Henry to care for his fifteen-year-old brother, Thomas. The two of them had to do the planting and run a gristmill. They had managed and were now grown men, and the threat of losing everything they had worked all their lives for weighed heavily on his mind.

The trail Henry was traveling went toward an old logging road that dead-ended at the base of a mountain, due to a spur. The only way out was through thick timbers and underbrush and he could hear the sound of several horses approaching.

Greater Love Hath No Man

Like a flash, he quickly spurred his big gray into the timbers and down the logging spur. As the horses came nearer, the sound of sabers clashing against the rider's stirrups made Henry's heart pound like a drum. With a lump in his throat, he watched as the West Virginia First Cavalry passed by.

Henry knew if he were caught they would arrest him on sight. The conscription act that Congress had recently ratified declaring that all men between twenty and forty-five years of age would serve in the military, gave them reason enough, and if they knew of his recent involvement it would be prison for sure.

When the troops rode out of sight, Henry waited several minutes before traveling on. He glanced around, looking at the terrain and the size of the trees. It all reminded him of his youth and of how he and his father cut timbers for lumber to build their barn. They had dragged logs from the woods on a track such as this one... perhaps even this exact one.

Convinced the troops were out of the area Henry guided his horse down the main trail. He soon came to another trail with which he was more familiar. Warming his backside at the fireplace in Butcher's Inn was a pleasant thought, but it was still a few miles down the road. With luck, he would make it in time for supper. He remembered that this particular track led to the back of the barn at Butcher's Inn, so he continued to follow the track in pursuit of rest and food.

By the time Henry got there, the tavern was already full. He could tell from the number of horses in the front, as well as from the sound of the fiddles and banjoes being played loudly to be heard over the noisy crowd.

Dismounting carefully, he kept a wary eye on the back door, just in case word had reached the Federals about the skirmish in the woods earlier. Henry did not need to answer any questions right now.

The barn door squealed in loud protest as it swung open. An old, former slave known only as Nigger Sam gave a toothless grin as Henry led his mare inside. Sam had on the same clothes he had worn the last time Henry saw him. The only difference was that his shoes had newspaper sticking in the holes to keep the cold out.

"You gonna wan me to stable yo hoss, massuh Henry," asked Sam, "whiles you goes inside?"

Henry shook his head, smiling, "Ain't ready for that just yet, Sam," he said as he led his horse to a stall that needed to be cleaned. "Bring that light, and help me pull down some hay," he called to Sam. Henry removed the mare's wet tack and threw it across a sawhorse. Tossing Sam a silver dollar, Henry said, "How about getting her some grain and giving her a good rub down?"

"Yassuh," mumbled Sam as he began the chores. "You be sure that money gets into the right hands, too, Sam, and I don't mean *your* right hand."

As Sam rubbed the mare, he glanced at Henry. "Dey is a lots of Yankees in dere if you be thinking on goin' inside, suh. If'n you wants, dis ol nigguh will sho be happy to go fetch you a cup from de kitchen, suh."

When Henry didn't answer, but rather started toward the back door, Sam muttered, "I reckon as how you gonna be staying out here wit yo mare and Nigguh Sam tonight, I reckon I best git you a place to lay."

Henry stepped in the back door of the tavern and warily scanned the crowd. The bar was full of travelers who were cussing the weather, drinking, and each trying to talk above the other.

He went to the next room and stood at a table where people were seated and eating quietly. A young man with a missing leg pushed his crutch out of the way and motioned for Henry to join him. As Henry sat, he scanned the room, and even though it was crowded, Henry still spotted a

Greater Love Hath No Man

group of Union officers sitting in a corner, drinking beer and laughing. One of them was also searching the crowd.

Henry slowly rose and walked to the bar where he ordered a cup of coffee. He left a half-dime on the bar and eased out the back door to make his way back to the barn. Old Sam was there to meet Henry. He was waving a lantern and motioning him to the back of the barn where he had piled up some hay for Henry's bed.

"I spread yo bed roll here fo you to sleep on, suh. Ah tol' you dey was a bunch of dem Yankees inside!"

"Yeah, you told me," answered Henry. "and Sam?"

"Yassuh?"

"Thanks."

Sam shuffled his feet and blew out the lantern, leaving the barn as dark as a cypress swamp on a moonless night. When old Caleb Butcher built this barn, he built it to last forever. It was made from virgin oak and was air tight. The only place cold wind could come in was through the swinging doors in the front, and as long as Sam remembered to keep a fire in the old Franklin stove, it was quite comfortable inside.

Henry lay in the dark thinking about his family.

His two daughters were undoubtedly piled up in bed with their mother, trying to stay warm. He wondered about the trip he was taking and the reasons for it. What if this was just a rumor? He drifted off to sleep with these questions unanswered.

Henry was not aware of the new snow that had fallen overnight. At dawn, a Rhode Island Red rooster announced the coming of the sun and ordered the world to awaken. "Damn rooster," thought Henry as he lay there, collecting his thoughts.

His eyes were closed, as if he were asleep. A nudge on his foot brought Henry full awake as his hand came from under the blanket with a .44 pointed at Sam's belly.

From the sound of old Sam breaking wind, one could assume he was rather frightened at the sight of the big gun.

Henry lowered the pistol, and Sam muttered, "Dey be a bucket of water over by de grain bin if you cares to wash up a bit. You may have to break de ice off'n it though. I got yo hoss saddled and ready to go an' a cup of hot coffee to staht yo day."

"I don't have any more silver dollars, Sam, so you can quit trying to be so nice," grumbled Henry.

"Don't matter none nohow cause when ol Nigguh Sam like somebody, he like'em an' I sho nuff like you, Massuh Henry. You and dat big old gray hoss I'd know from anywhere. Miss Bertha ax me to fetch you. She want you to take brefist wif her."

Holding his coffee with a wool mitten, Henry sipped the hot liquid and wondered why Miss Bertha wanted him to eat breakfast with her.

Ignoring Sam, Henry said, "It turned off colder last night, didn't it Sam? Looks like some new snow, too."

Sam nodded and continued mucking out the stall where the gray mare had been. "Sam, have you heard anything about Virginia not being Virginia any more and us being called West Virginia, now?"

Sam put his rake down and scratched his wooly head as he walked over to Henry, "Nawsuh, massuh Henry, I ain' heard dat but you knows dat old Virginny is gonna stay Virginny no matter what dem white folk in Washington does."

"Well," answered Henry, "them white folks in Washington made you a free man with Mr. Lincoln's Proclamation thing."

Sam went back to his raking the stall saying, "Yassuh, indeed he did. Thank de Lawd fo dat."

As Henry approached the door of the barn, he turned to Sam.

"Hey Sam. Let's have some breakfast together." He took a strip of beef jerky from his saddlebag and cut it in half, sharing it with the former slave.

"Why thank you, massuh Henry, and God bless you suh."

Chapter two

The screeching of a red tail hawk, circling above, brought attention to the blue sky of Virginia. Henry paused to watch, amazed by the spectacular touch-and-go tactics, as the hawk gracefully swooped up its prey and carried the victim to her nest.

Bertha Butcher was busy sweeping off the back porch while waiting for Henry to ride by. He ignored her as he guided his gray mare away from the barn.

"Henry Watkins, you might ought to hear what I have to tell you before you ride outta this yard," she quipped.

Henry paused his horse and looked in her direction.

"The Yankee cavalry has set an ambush for your brother and his bunch over at Deer Run; just thought you should know", she said, quietly.

"Why Bertha, did you get religion?" Henry asked.

"I shouldn't have said a damn word and went on and let them catch the both of you bastards," she responded harshly.

"Now, now, Bertha, don't drop your bonnet in the mud," Henry said smiling as he rode on.

With caution, he rode to a trail that ran along at an angle toward the mountains. Underbrush was so thick at times he would dismount and walk his horse through areas that a rabbit would have difficulty traveling. He knew that if he stayed on the main pike, conscription brokers would await him like bandits.

The sun was high when he reached a trail that led to Carter Town. It was warmer now, causing little streams of water from melting snow. Sunbeams reflecting from clumps of snow in the trees were beautiful with Christmas Rose and other perennials blooming along the hillsides, blooming as though they were trying to push spring in all at once.

Riding near the ridge and looking out across a little valley, Henry thought, an artist could win a prize by capturing junipers among the pines, creating such a beautiful green background for the profusion of beautyberries that ran along the trail up ahead.

Soon witch hazel plants would be in bloom along the hillsides, giving the world a sweet fragrance, along with snowdrops and wild irises with their blue tops.

Glancing downward Henry could see Butcher's Inn and any movement when anyone who came or left.

Bertha was not one to be trusted and most people who knew her also knew of her double-dealing both sides of any argument.

It had been three months since Lincoln freed their slaves, and only old Nigger Sam and two more stayed, while all the others left for other unknown places. Henry watched Bertha's place for a short time to assure himself he was not being followed.

As he neared a bend in the trail, he heard the noise of a wagon and people shouting at their animals. He rode on and found there were a number of large freight wagons loaded down with people and others filled with furniture and personal items. When the last wagon came close enough to where Henry could speak to someone, he hailed the driver to stop. There was a woman driving the team of mules. Her daughter sat next to her, holding a shotgun.

"I mean you no harm, ma'am, but wanted to know if you have come from Carter Town," Henry asked softly.

Spitting out a mouthful of tobacco juice and wiping her mouth, she replied, "ain't much left of Carter Town, if'n that's where yew going".

"What happened?" Henry asked.

"Yankees is what happened! They come shooting, killing folk, burning down everything that was standing! We barely got out with our lives."

"When did this take place?" Henry asked.

"Just as it was getting dark. They come whooping and hollering like ruffians dressed in uniforms instead of soldiers. Not like our boys in gray, giving lady folk respect, but more like demons wanting to burn everything and kill all the men folk or haul them off to prison. Said they were all copperheads and just shot them down in cold blood."

Weeping while she finished telling Henry the story, she yelled at he mules, "Mules, get up there," as she cracked a whip across their backs.

Henry moved out of the way and traveled on toward Carter Town thinking about what he had just heard. His mind went back to the time when he voted to keep Virginia in the union while others wanted otherwise. He was a son and grandson of patriots, and to think his countrymen could do such a thing was beyond his comprehension.

As he rode nearer to Carter Town, he met others leaving. Expressions on their faces told Henry the woman was telling the truth. Carter Town was known for harboring Confederate sympathizers as well as southern guerilla forces. John Carter was his only hope of finding his brother, and if he were too late he would have to try something different.

Just before entering the charred remains of Carter Town, a small white frame house sat unharmed, beneath a grove of pin oak trees. Henry stopped and tied his horse's reins to a low hanging limb.

Walking up to the front door with his hand on his navy colt pistol he shouted, "Anybody here?" No answer came. Still he shouted once more, "Anybody home?" Again there was no answer.

He walked upon the porch and turned the door knob when an old woman holding a shotgun greeted him saying, "What yew want here? I ain't got nuthin for yew. Them damn Yankees took all I had."

"Ma'am, you got me wrong; I come in peace looking for John Carter. Would you know where I might find him?"

"Got no time fer yew," she said, slamming the door in his face. Henry thought for a moment and knocked on the door again.

This time the old lady opened the door and shouted, "If'n yew don't git, I'll blast you with this here shotgun! Now I mean it!"

Henry knew she was serious and walked away mumbling under his breath, "Hope I can make it out of here in one piece." Slowly mounting his horse and tipping his hat as he rode off he said, "Keep that handy lady; I think you'll be all right." Little did he know that he had just visited John Carter's mother.

At the local cemetery several people were gathered, praying and burying their dead. Henry stopped his horse near a stone fence, which separated him from the group. While he watched and waited for them to finish, a small boy approached and asked, "Are you a Yankee?"

Henry thought for a minute and then answered, "No son, I'm a farmer."

Before the boy ran away, Henry asked, "Reckon you might know how I can find Mr. John Carter?"

"Sure," he replied. "that's him reading the bible in front of those people."

Henry dismounted, and pulling his hat off, he walked slowly to the group. He paused for a moment to keep from attracting attention to himself. But John Carter was well aware of the stranger in their midst. Henry had been noticed long before he stopped at the fence.

Henry waited until the service was over and then walked to where the man was reading the bible. "You John Carter?" he asked.

Pausing before he answered, the man replied quietly, "Yes sir, I be John Carter."

John was a former Indian fighter, and with a hard-bitten attitude showing in his face, one would know he was all business. His tawny mustache and cold gray eyes made him look like something out of the Lewis and Clark expedition. He was a soft-spoken, good natured and sober man. He wore an old hunting shirt, and his ancient black corduroy breeches were tucked into the tops of his cowhide boots. A big pipe and a smoking tobacco pouch were sticking out his shirt pockets.

"I'm Captain Thomas Watkins' brother. Would you know how I might get in touch with him?" Henry inquired.

"There is a small frame house just as you come into town, sitting back under a clump of pin oaks; you ride down there, and I will be along directly. We can talk then, but right now I need to finish burying these folks."

"I think I have already met the lady of the house. Why don't I help you here and we can go together." Henry answered.

"So, you've met Maw," John chuckled. He called out to two men lowering a casket, "Tom, you and Horace take over 'till I get back. I won't be long."

Henry and John Carter mounted their horses and rode to the little house.

When they stepped on the porch, the old woman met them, still holding the shotgun. "Maw, put that thing away," John barked at his mother, "this here is Captain Watkins' brother."

With a deep sigh of relief she replied, "Cain't be to keerful with folks nowadays."

The two men sat down at a table and began talking while the old woman poured them hot coffee.

"You know, when those fellows hit us it was like they knew just when to do it," Carter began. "They came riding in about dusk, and we was so surprised that nobody had a chance to organize any kind of defense. Before anyone knowed it, the whole town was full of Yankees. When I heard all the shootin', I grabbed my rifle and rode as fast as I could to the edge of town.

"I could see that they had done took control of everything and with what little light that was left, I shot one Yankee out of his saddle. I didn't kill him though; 'stead, old man Prather went over and crushed his skull with the butt of his gun.

"Two other Yankees rode up and killed Prather and burned his store down. They even shot Mrs. Prather when she come runnin' out the burnin' building. She didn't die though, thank the lord. Old doc Glass patched her up, and now she's stayin' at the church, along with a lot of others."

"Where was my brother during this time?" Henry asked.

"Cap'n Watkins and his troops was across the river. They had intended to come to our aid, but them marauding Yankee devils had done cut the rope to the ferry. They was miles from the next crossing," explained John as best he could. "What little resistance we offered, along with your brother's troops shootin' into the streets, caused the cowards to give up the fight before they was finished. We killed as many of those bastards as we could see by firelight from the burnin' buildings."

"Do you reckon my brother will ford and come here?" Henry asked.

"Naw, I figure he's crossed Deer Run by now and is runnin' down that bunch. And woe be unto them when he do catch 'em. All hell is gonna bust loose." John sipped his coffee and packed his corncob pipe with homegrown tobacco. As he drew on the pipe, he squinted at Henry. "How come you gotta get to him in such a hurry, anyhow?" He asked.

Henry jumped up from his chair, startling the old woman. "Did you say Deer Run?" Henry asked, growing pale, remembering Bertha's warning about the ambush planned at Deer Run. "How far is it from here? I have got to get there, and I hope I'm not too late."

Greater Love Hath No Man

Chapter three

When Henry walked out of the Carter's house, John followed him, knocking the ash from his pipe in the palm of his hand. Before mounting his big gray, Henry turned and said, "I want to thank you and your mother. I only wish I could have been here sooner."

The old woman walked out the house carrying something wrapped in a cloth. Handing it to John, she quietly said, "Give this to 'im," and walked back to the house. John handed the parcel to Henry.

"Probably some salt pork and bread", said John, "She's good about things like that. And by the way, there is something you still ought to know before you start off half-cocked. Just at the edge of town, on the right, there is a big red oak tree standin' in front of what use to be Lancaster's General store. You see, this is not the first time those Federal boys have been here. They are led by a Major by the name of Simmons who has sworn to hang your brother and my two boys from that very tree and leave 'em there until the flesh has rotted off their bones. And if anybody cut 'em down, he would hang that person next to 'em. But that would be over my dead body."

Henry looked at John with understanding as John continued, "Now, you will need to take that trail that runs under that big oak. You go south about four miles or better and you should come to a small settlement of Scottish/ Irish people. They all are northern patriots. People around here call 'em purple corn meal folks. You'll find your way from there."

"Mr. Carter, thank your mother for me. It has been a pleasure to meet you folks. I'm sure we will see one another again," said Henry as he rode off.

When he arrived at the red oak, he paused for a moment looking up at its limbs. "We'll just have to see about that," mumbled Henry, as he guided his horse onto the trail.

The wind had died to a whisper by the time he reached the timberline, and the sun was hanging low in the western sky. Henry knew if he didn't make it to the settlement before sundown, he would be making camp in the woods. The trail was narrow in places and quite dangerous.

When he would come to openings where snow had melted, making the mud deep and slippery. He carefully walked his mount through these places, preparing to dismount in a hurry if she slipped. After a short while, he came to another opening where several horses had passed in the same direction he was traveling.

This must be where that bunch came through, he thought. Knowing that if it was the Federals, they had probably already paid the settlement a visit, or perhaps they were still there. With caution he rode on, looking ahead, glancing at both sides of the trail, prepared for anything. The need of warning his brother was imperative, but the pace of reaching him would be much slower now. He didn't know the terrain, and if he were caught, they would arrest him as a draft dodger.

He searched the heavens for any sign of clouds knowing that clear skies would bring colder temperatures, as well as enough light to see if any troops were there. As he rode down a steep, winding hill he smelled wood smoke. Stopping his horse, he dismounted and tied her reins to a branch and eased along the trail until it came to a dell. Just a few yards away was a Federal picket guard standing by a fire.

Henry carefully backed away without being noticed and crept back to his mount. *Well Simmons, now I know where you are,* he said to himself. He still wasn't sure just how far he was from the settlement, but one thing was for sure: the Federals weren't at Deer Run.

Off the trail, underbrush was so thick it would be very difficult to go around. He would have to go back up the trail, where he first saw the Federal horses' hoof prints and try to get around them from another direction. Any decision he made would have to be made soon, because the sun was beginning to set.

After several attempts at entering the brush, he realized that the risk wasn't worth losing his mount or perhaps his own life. He decided to wait them out. He tied his gray once again behind a brush top concealed from the trail and walked back to where he saw the picket guard. Henry was high above the guard, which made it possible to see down into the dell and to monitor every movement.

He rested his back in a sitting position against a big white oak tree, smiling as he mumbled, "Well Simmons, I see your tent down there, and it looks like we're gonna spend the night together."

Henry was right about the clearing of the sky bringing in a full moon, and right about it becoming colder. About midnight, while the boys dressed in blue were lying around warm fires and the Major in his warm tent, Henry was shaking from the cold. At times, he would nod off to sleep, but he was determined to stick it out. He thought about his blankets in his bedroll, but the guard had looked up, seemingly right at Henry at least twice and had not seen him. He didn't want to chance the third, so he simply went without.

Just before dawn, he was roused by the cracking noise of twigs breaking. Down the slope, he saw two figures moving through the timbers. Then three more. To his right, several more crouched closer to the Union camp. From his position, he could see everything.

The picket guard that had stood by the fire during the night was now lying on the ground. Not more than ten feet away, a solider dressed in butternut gray passed by. He was wearing a plume feather in his hat and was carrying a carbine.

Henry's cold shakes had stopped suddenly, warmed by the hot blood pumping from his pounding heart and rushing through his body. He didn't dare move a muscle but watched as the shadows moved slowly toward the campsite. This should be interesting, Henry thought, as he watched each man pick a position for the moment of surprise.

He knew all hell was about to break loose and he was sitting in a location where anything could happen. If I'm gonna be in this, he thought, it will be riding, not dodging bullets under some old oak tree. He quickly scurried up the slope to the place where he had tied his horse.

Sitting there, holding Henry's big gray by her bridle, was John Carter. "You'll be needing her, I'm sure, in a few minutes," John said excitedly. Henry was shocked to see John, and before he could get a word out the shooting began. "We'd best wait until it's over," John said calmly.

Henry thought of how close he was to meeting Major Simmons face-to-face and smiled. "You knew about this all the time didn't you?" Henry asked sharply.

"Couldn't take a chance on you being caught and them getting it out of you, so its better this way," answered John. "Besides, it worked and that's all that matters, ain't it?"

When the shooting stopped, John spoke quietly, "Let's go. I think someone wants to see you."

Riding down the slope and into the dell, Henry could see the results of the surprise attack. Major Simmons and his twenty-two men had just felt the impact of what southern cavalry on foot could do. Leaving twelve Union troopers dead and two more mortally wounded, including Major Simmons.

Close quarters fighting was something Thomas and his men had been experiencing for the past three years.

The Carter boys were guarding prisoners when their father and Henry rode up. "Mr. Watkins, I want you to meet my two sons, Chadwick and Eli," John said.

Nodding his head at Henry, Eli spoke "If'n you be looking for the Captain, he's over where that Yankee Major is laying. He caught one in the guts. Probably ain't gonna make it, but it serves him right. I hope the bastard dies."

John asked, "How many did we lose, son?"

"Not sure, Paw. The sergeant will let us know later," Chadwick responded.

Henry left the three talking and rode to where his brother Thomas stood, looking down at the union Major. While waiting patiently until Thomas was through, he looked out across the area and saw men rounding up horses and their bounty. Two Confederates soldiers were digging a trench that would serve as a mass grave for the dead. Major Simmons was propped up against a tree, so he could watch as Thomas' men dragged the dead soldiers. Stripping them of all their personal items, they tossed them into the trench.

Engrossed with his men and their achievement, Thomas was reminded by his sergeant that his brother, Henry, awaited him.

When Thomas saw Henry mounted on the big gray horse, he calmly walked over to him smiling. "Hell of a way to see a loved one," he called.

Henry quickly dismounted and stood before his brother. The two men stood the same size and resembled bears in a hugging contest when they embraced. If the two were in the same uniforms, they would look like twins. Even John Carter and several of the men remarked on how they looked alike. "Lets go into the tent and talk," Thomas suggested. "God, it's good to see you."

It seemed that questions just rolled from his lips, causing Henry to interrupt, saying, "Whoa! Wait a minute! One at a time!"

Thomas paused for a moment and then asked, "What are you doing here? You came to warn me about Deer Run, right?"

Henry never said a word, but simply stared at Thomas. Henry's mind flashed back to when they were small boys and how they would listen to their grandfather tell stories of how cold he got at Valley Forge and how his grandmother would correspond with Abigail Adams.

What has happened? Why are we fighting each other? Where is this leading us? Those were the questions that were in Henry's head that pushed all others aside. In response to Thomas' questions Henry nodded his head.

"You get good care from old Nigger Sam?" Thomas asked.

"You know about my trip to Bertha Butcher's place, I see. Tell me brother, how do you know so much about my whereabouts, and why did I have to come to John Carter's place to find out about you after all this time?"

Thomas replied with another question, "Was that you up on that ridge at Butcher's holler, helping out those boys that the Yanks had pinned down? Shooting into their backside was plenty smart."

"I didn't hit anyone, just scared 'em a little," Henry answered.

"Well brother whether you like it, or not, you have just joined the ranks of the terrible Johnny Rebs."

Greater Love Hath No Man

Chapter four

The brothers' reunion was interrupted by a dispatch rider who carried a message from Thomas' commanding officer. The note informed him that the "gallant" General Penham had been killed.

Staring at Henry, Thomas remarked, "This is bad news. One of our finest Generals has been killed at Kellysville". With the note in his hand, Thomas walked outside the tent and looked up toward the heavens and uttered a quiet prayer.

Henry followed, not saying a word, but observing every move his brother made.

Greater Love Hath No Man

The sergeant waited until he was finished before speaking, "Begging the Captain's pardon, sir, but the Yankee trooper just died, and that Yankee Major keeps asking for you. Shall I put a bullet in his head and put him out of his misery?"

Thomas paused for a moment then gently responded, "No sergeant, I'll see the Major. Excuse me, brother, while I attend to this," nodding to Henry as he walked over to where the Major lay.

The Major's body was cold and frail. Speaking barely above a whisper, he said, "Captain, remember those prisoners are good boys and were just following orders. Treat them as you would want me to treat yours, and as for me, Captain, I know that I don't have much longer, so finish me personally, so that I can be buried with my troopers."

"And why should I do this?" Thomas asked.

"Professional courtesy, sir. Just call it professional courtesy," Simmons whispered.

Henry watched to see how his brother would respond to the Major's request.

Slowly, Thomas raised his pistol toward Simmons head. After hesitating for a long moment, he lowered his revolver and placed it back into its holster.

"Sergeant, have the men ready to move out in ten minutes; we are taking the Major with us. Have two men gather up the prisoners and take them to headquarters. Also, tell that dispatch rider I'm sending a message back with him. Understood?"

"Yes, sir!" came the sergeant's response.

Thomas walked back to where Henry waited. "The men want you to ride with us after what you did at Butchers holler. I'll send a dispatch to Mr. Davis asking that he give you a commission, if you wish."

Henry responded sharply, "My feelings haven't changed one bit. We already went through this, when this madness started."

"Then pray tell me why you got involved helping those boys out then?" Thomas asked. Shaking his head, and walking back to the tent Thomas remarked, "Stubborn, stubborn, just plain damn, stubborn. What do these bastards have to do: come burn you out and kill your wife and kids before you learn?

"We are not with General Washington, and we are sure as hell not with Father fighting Mexicans, dammit. We are engaged in an all out war here in your front yard. Does one of these damn Yankees have to put a lead ball in you before you accept it? Dammit brother, you owe it to your family if nothing else," Thomas demanded.

Henry stood silently, remembering the days when they would work together and talk about how much land they would own. He thought of how they had made plans of raising the finest corn and sugar cane crops in the state.

Thomas watched the men gather the equipment for departure while he cooled his temper some. He said, "Let's walk over here, while the men take down this tent. I want to show you something."

He and Henry walked to where the union prisoners had covered the bodies of their fallen comrades.

Thomas looked at one of the prisoners and asked, "Do any of you know why you are here on Virginia soil, killing innocent people and burning their homes?"

One of the prisoners responded, "Just following orders, Captain, just following orders."

Henry watched as the expressions on their faces changed when Thomas asked another question, "Where you from solider?"

"New York, sir. Gunridge, New York," he replied.

"You a farm boy, son?" Thomas asked.

"Yes, sir." he answered.

"You ever have anyone from Virginia come burn you out and kill your kin?" Thomas asked.

Henry knew this was for his benefit, but in his heart it didn't change a thing. Not even when Thomas' final question caused the young solider to cry.

"Then why are you fellows here, invading our state, doing to our people what you wouldn't want done to yours?"

A Union sergeant glanced over at his dying Major and shouted, "Because that traitor Lee would be at my house doing the same thing, if we let him."

Thomas knew this was leading nowhere. Slowly walking away, he replied, "Well sergeant, that's gonna be hard to do where your going."

Both brothers walked back to where the tent had stood moments before. It was Henry that broke the silence by saying "Brother, I need to know what to do about our property if northern Virginia goes back into the Union."

Thomas sharply replied, "It has already been done, according to my information, but no official word has been given to that effect. So, brother, that's another thing you might want to consider. They're gonna take our land and might be doing it now, as we speak."

The sergeant brought both men their horses and when Thomas mounted his horse, he looked deep into Henry's black eyes and said "You know, losing my Elizabeth and the baby caused me to build my life around you and your family; then this blasted war came. Neighbors we thought were our friends came stealing and telling lies on us, making life difficult. All because Father served under Jefferson Davis down in Mexico.

"No, sir, brother, those same neighbors are going to be the people that will burn your place and kill your family before this thing is over, if you don't watch it. Go home Henry, while you can. Go home and stand guard over your place, and when those wonderful neighbors we gave food and shelter to during their hard times turn and sell you out for thirty pieces of silver, think on our little talk."

Henry watched them ride toward the settlement. Thomas rode out front, wearing three beautiful plume feathers in his hat, which blew in the breeze. Henry was aware of the disappointment and hurt that his brother felt. He mounted his big gray horse and while pondering the things Thomas had said, John Carter rode over to his side.

"Hate to see those boys ride out, knowing we might never see them again," John remarked.

"What will they do with Simmons?" Henry asked.

"Probably leave him to die with his own supporters if he ain't already dead. Why you so concerned about what they do with that fella?" John asked.

"No particular reason," answered Henry, "just curious, I reckon."

After a long glance at Henry, John said, "I'll be headin' back home, now. Figure you fixin' to do the same. If you care to ride along with me, I'd be pleased. Besides, I have something to show you, if you be interested."

"Why not," Henry replied, "got to pick up the same trail that heads east, anyway, and besides, fighting all this underbrush would be a chore."

John was hoping that Henry would get a good look at the damage Simmons had caused, as well as meet some of the victims and hear what they had to say. It was obvious that Henry was having mixed emotions about everything, and if John's plan worked, they'd make it back to his place late enough that Henry would probably stay the night and get an early start the next

Morning.

As the two men rode on, Henry reached back, his long fingers fumbling with the straps on his saddlebags. He was trying to work it open so he could get to what Maw Carter had given him. Seeing he would have to stop and get off his horse to do so, he called out, "John, hold up a minute, what do ya' say we try some of the vittles your mother sent with us."

"Sounds good. Let's head for that clump of oaks and make camp for awhile," John said and smiled. As his mind churned with the need for a short nap after they ate, he thought this would put them just right for his plan.

Chapter five

John smiled, knowing that after a short nap they would get to Carter Town at just about dark, but Henry wasn't about to let that happen. When they finished Henry walked to a brush top and relieved himself, while leaving John sounding like an old she bear.

When Henry returned to the camp site, he picked up a pine twig and stuck it under John's nose, waking him with a snort.

"I take it we need to git," John said.

"Yep, I got a long way to go, and I haven't seen my family in several days. They are probably starting to worry about me, by now." Henry answered.

Both men mounted and rode on. The sun was low when they reached the edge of Carter Town.

"Before you head out toward home, there is someone I would like for you to meet; that is if you have time," John said.

"No, I don't mind, but I really need to get on down the trail if I want to make it home by dark tomorrow," Henry answered. They came to a church with a sign over the door that read "Community Chapel." The church was made of brick. John, along with many others believed this served as a deterrent to Yankees torches.

The two men dismounted and tied their horses to a nearby rail. A white-haired man greeted them at the door, "Gentlemen, it's so good to see you."

John responded, "Dr. Glass, this is Henry Watkins, Captain Watkins' brother from over around Mineral Wells."

"Did you say Mineral Wells?" Dr. Glass asked.

Henry nodded his head. "My oldest brother is a doctor over there. Perhaps you know him," the doctor said.

"In fact, I do. Old Doc Glass delivered both my girls. I guess I've known Dr. Glass most of my life. Does he not have a daughter named Rosemary?" Asked Henry.

"Yes," answered the doctor. "she went away to medical school in New York, the last I heard."

"Well, Doc, she's back home now living with her folks and helping her father," Henry replied.

"You gentlemen please excuse me. I have patients to tend. Watkins, it was a pleasure. Hope you stick around awhile, there's a lot of things I would like to discuss with you, if you have the time," Dr. Glass said.

John Carter was delighted at the direction in which the conversation was going.

"Henry," he exclaimed, "I want you to meet some other good people." He walked over to a woman who held a baby. John introduced them as his daughter and grandbaby. "I had just finished burying her husband when you rode up," John said.

A small boy, about twelve years old, approached John, asking, "Grampaw, did y'all catch them Yankees?"

John smiled, "Yes, son. We got 'em." He knelt and whispered in the boy's ear, "I want you do me a favor. Go out and take my horse and that big gray out front to the stable and unsaddle them and give the some grain."

The boy did as he was asked. Scampering out the door, he looked back and said to Henry "I'll see you, farmer."

John looked at Henry and asked, "What's that all about?"

"Met him at the cemetery yesterday, just before I met you," Henry replied.

One of the ladies passing by called, "There's hot soup on the stove, if you want it."

Both men looked at each other, and smiling, walked to the stove. "I take it you'll bed down with us and get an early start in the morning," John remarked.

Looking at John with a big grin, Henry said, "Something like that."

Henry went outside the next morning. The weather had become much warmer and had caused the remainder of the snow to form small pools of water in various places. Henry quickly discovered this fact when he once slipped, almost falling.

Trying to regain his composure and straightening his hat, he heard someone chuckle behind him. He looked back to see who might have thought he was such a buffoon and saw an elegant lady of class. Her shiny black hair was parted in the center of her head. The length was wrapped and secured in a bun, which made the fullness of her face sparkle like sunshine on water.

"Ma'am," Henry said, removing his hat.

Wondering whether she was afraid to walk off the wooden planks and cross the road, Henry asked, "Are you trying to get across or just interested in seeing someone make a fool himself?"

"Neither," she laughed, "I was sent to ask if you would like to take a bath and freshen up before you start home. God knows you could use one."

Returning her smile, Henry asked, "And who is this person that is so interested in my personal hygiene?"

Giving Henry another beautiful smile, she answered, "Dr. Glass has invited you to his home. You are Captain Watkins' brother, aren't you?"

"Yes ma'am, but may I ask your name?"

Brushing Henry's question aside she said, "I am told your name is Henry Watkins. That is right, I presume."

"You speak as though you may have come from up north somewhere. New York, no doubt." Henry responded.

"Mr. Watkins, if you will just follow me to Dr. Glass' home, we can talk more privately," she said.

"Ma'am, what I have to say don't need any privacy, and if I'm going to walk with such a beautiful lady, I should at least know her name, don't you think?" Henry asked again.

"Caroline," she said and smiled. "Dr. Glass is my father, so if you don't mind, may we walk to the house now?" She asked.

"Just lead the way, Miss Caroline. I'm your obedient servant," said Henry, grinning like an idiot. The plank they walked on was so narrow that Henry had to follow her.

The Glass family lived in a large antebellum house, sitting near the top of a small knoll, which gave the impression of prosperity. When Caroline and Henry reached the house, a well-dressed light-skinned Negro man met them at the door and said, "Miss Caroline, your father awaits you in his study."

Henry was amazed how well spoken he was. "This is Bonner, Mr. Watkins; he will show you to your bath, and then if you like you may dine with us," Caroline said and smiled

Henry was overwhelmed with such luxury and manners. Having mud still on his boots and clothes made him feel inferior, but he followed Bonner to a large room across the hallway.

Just before they entered, Caroline motioned to the servant with her fingers in a scissor-cutting motion and said, "Bonner, see that Mama Bonner gives Mr. Watkins a trim." Then, giving Henry a smile she said, "don't worry Mr. Watkins. Mama Bonner has plenty of experience in such matters."

The two men went in the room and closed the door. Two young Negro boys were filling a wooden tub with hot water for Henry's bath. A door on the other side of the room was the entrance for the young boys. When one of them would bring a bucket of water, Henry could hear giggling. Bonner went to the door, gave them a stern look, and the giggling stopped.

While Henry bathed, Bonner took his boots and clothes into another room to be cleaned. When Bonner returned them, his boots shined and his clothing was clean and pressed.

"Bonner, these boots didn't look this good when I bought them three years ago," Henry said and smiled.

"Thank you, sir. I do try."

Placing Henry's trousers and shirt in a straight back chair and handing Henry a towel, Bonner said, "When you get dressed, Mama Bonner will give you your trim."

"How long were you a slave?" Henry asked.

"The Glass family bought me over thirty-five years ago and gave me freedom that very day," answered Bonner. "I have lived here since that time. Mama Bonner and my twelve children are free born; they have never been slaves."

"So you are free to come and go as you please?" Henry asked.

"Yes sir, this is my family's home, and we are paid each year by Dr. Glass and have always been." Bonner answered. "I have family in New York and go there occasionally but not since the war started."

Their conversation was interrupted when Mama Bonner knocked to ask whether Henry was finished with his bath.

"Tell her to come on in, Bonner. I'm ready." Henry said. Sitting in the straight back chair with the towel draped around his shoulders, Henry waited patiently.

Mama Bonner was a quiet lady, and judging from her size she never went hungry. Henry sat as obedient as a schoolboy and nearly drifted to sleep.

When she finished, she removed the towel from Henry's shoulders and held a mirror so that Henry could see himself. She said, "There, Mr. Watkins, you should feel much lighter now."

Henry just grinned, "My Mildred couldn't have done a better job."

From the doorway, Bonner summoned Henry to come with him. "If you don't mind, sir," he said softly, "Dr. Glass would like to see you now."

Henry followed Bonner down the hallway to the dining room. Bonner opened the doors and escorted Henry to a long table. Already seated at the head of the table was Dr. Glass, Caroline at his right and John Carter at his left. That left an empty seat between him and three other well-dressed men. Bonner led Henry to the empty seat.

Henry's heart was pounding so hard he was afraid Bonner could hear it. As he sat, he remembered his father's reading of the scriptures, "The rich man's wealth is his strong city; the destruction of the poor is their poverty."

The meal in front of Henry was fit for a king as far as he was concerned. He was served a bowl of Hopping John stew, which was well known in this area, along with a variety of vegetables that had been stored in the cellar.

Two young, very well-mannered light-skinned Negro girls, dressed alike, served the guests.

Henry was amazed by their cleanliness. *No doubt, these girls must be Bonner's*, he thought.

Dr. Glass introduced Henry to his other guests, saying, "Gentlemen, this is Mr. Henry Watkins, brother of Captain Watkins of the Virginia volunteers." He went on to introduce each one of the three men as the mayor, John Bedford; Reverend Charles of the Methodist faith; and Horace Whitten, the local undertaker. Then he said, "I think you know Mr. Carter and my daughter."

"Yes sir, I do. Gentlemen, it's a pleasure," Henry smiled.

The food was delicious. It was Henry's first home-cooked meal in four days. Henry couldn't take his eyes off Caroline. Her presence was comforting to everyone.

After the meal, Bonner came in carrying a tray of short drinking glasses and a bottle of Napoleon brandy.

"Gentlemen, I would like to propose a toast in honor of Captain Thomas Watkins and his gallant men. They saved this home and many more with their rapid fire from across the river, keeping the Federals out of this section of town," Dr. Glass said, raising his glass. Everyone stood lifting his or her glasses saying, "Hear, hear." After the toast, Dr. Glass asked the men to join him in the parlor for a smoke.

Noticing Caroline walking to the patio, Henry quickly said, "Gentlemen, I don't smoke. If you will excuse me, I will visit with Miss Caroline."

Greater Love Hath No Man

As the two walked out to the patio, she turned and said, "Why Mr. Watkins, it seems that you have followed me all day. But I must say that your appearance is much improved since we first met."

"You provided a wonderful meal, and it's not often that one meets such an attractive hostess. May I ask what this all about?" Henry asked nervously.

"John Carter tells me that you are married and have children. That is correct, isn't it?"

"That's correct," Henry answered. "You still haven't told me what this is all about. I'm impressed that you honor my brother, but that's far from the truth of the matter isn't it?" Henry asked.

Avoiding his question, she replied "Perhaps we should go back inside. There is a chill in the breeze."

He knew something was up, but whatever it was, he wasn't about to let it involve him. Henry walked beside her when they entered the house. He smiled and said, "You know, this is the first time I have walked beside you. If I may ask, why aren't you married? Is this a choice you've made or was it your father's?"

Stopping and looking straight at Henry, she explained, "My husband was killed at the start of the war; my last name is Fairchild."

Henry felt embarrassed and began to apologize.

With a mischievous grin she said, "No need to apologize; I should have made my self more plain when we met."

Henry thought to himself, *There is nothing plain about you, lady.*

John Carter and Reverend Charles entered the room talking about the weather and plans to start rebuilding Carter Town.

"Oh there you two are," the Reverend exclaimed. "Mrs. Fairchild, I never got a chance to tell you how radiant you look today. Will you be staying longer this time?"

Henry listened carefully to pick up any useful information.

"Mr. Watkins, if you are staying over it would be a pleasure having you at church Sunday."

"Thanks, Reverend," answered Henry. "If I was staying, I would be delighted, but I'll be going home shortly."

Excusing himself, the minister walked away. John Carter said, "I best be going, too. Got a lot of things to get done. By the way, Henry, may I speak to you in private?"

Caroline excused herself, leaving the two men to talk alone. "Henry, I believe I can trust you about something," John started. "Have you ever heard of a lady they call Wild Rose? Her real name is Rose O'Neal Greenhow."

Henry paused for moment thinking about John's question. "No, should I?" Before John responded, Dr. Glass approached, interrupting their conversation.

"Gentlemen, I'm needed. I have wounded to attend, so if you will excuse me; Mr. Watkins, thank you once again for coming. I hope to see you another time."

"Perhaps you will," Henry said and smiled.

"When I see your brother I will tell him of our meeting."

"That would be nice of you," Henry answered. The mayor followed the doctor outside and smiled at Henry while passing.

In Henry's mind, things were starting to baffle him. *First, I came to find my brother to get answers about our land, and then I wind up in a fire fight, causing me to take a side, which I had no intentions of doing. Next, I find myself in the company of a beautiful woman, and John Carter is standing here wanting to know if I know a woman. I think need to take Thomas' advice and go home.*

Greater Love Hath No Man

Henry looked at John and said "I have never heard of the person you mentioned, and I think I need to head home. So, John, maybe we will see one another, again."

Henry walked outside toward the stables and met a young light-skinned Negro boy leading his big gray horse, coming toward him. "Here's your horse, sir," the young man said.

Henry reached into his pocket and pulled out a half dime and handed it to the boy. "Oh no, sir, I'm not allowed to take anything. My father forbids such," he said.

"You are all right young man. You'll go far in this world." Henry smiled, then mounted and rode away.

John Carter stood at the door smoking his pipe and watching until Henry was out of sight.

Chapter six

The month of March left the state of Virginia like a lion, pushing April in like a lamb. Henry had watched the last migration flight of the Canadian honkers going north.

It was planting time, and the smell of fresh dirt being turned over made the people anxious to begin the spring work. They were busy, trying to dismiss the ongoing war and the inflated prices they paid at the local general stores.

This would be the time Henry would make his money. With corn meal costing anywhere from sixteen to three-hundred dollars per bushel and wheat at twenty dollars a barrel, there was no doubt in his mind where he would be for the next several months. His wife, Mildred, and his daughters would be raising a proper garden to provide their spending money as well.

Peas were bringing forty-eight dollars a bushel, and squash were fifty cents each. In addition, people would be in need of the mill and Henry's skill of grinding corn and sugar cane.

Yep, Henry thought, this should be a very good year.

Mildred Watkins was a petite woman with flaming red hair and green eyes. When she smiled, her face seemed to glow. Her freckles complemented her smooth complexion. Henry's two daughters, Violet and Gladys, were tomboys, always exploring their surroundings by climbing trees and building secret hiding places when Mildred had extra chores for them to do.

Violet was thirteen, and her hair was a flaming red like her mother's. Gladys was eleven, with jet black hair, and resembled her father. Both were as energetic as any boy was and could ride horses like the wind.

Henry knew he had a beautiful family. They worked hard for what they had and were going to do everything in their power to keep it.

They were also aware of the conscription act and the effect it could have on them if conscription brokers found Henry.

The family was very cautious of everyone and quiet about their business. Strangers would come by to water their horses or inquire directions into Mineral Wells. They would always be spoken to from a distance.

Today was Sunday, and bells ringing at the church hurried the Watkins family along in preparing for their journey to town. People would come for miles to seek courage from the word of God, while others came to show off their new frocks.

Garibaldi skirts and dresses with puffed sleeves and military style shoulders with collars were in style. Men had a thing about top hats and derbies, especially with a frock coat, and accessories such as canes and suspenders. Ladies would show off their new bonnets and home-designed dresses that they had made during the winter, and this was usually the high point of their conversation.

After morning services, they would spread dinner on the ground and show off quilts and new patterns while the men pitched horseshoes or talked about current events.

Church services offered peace of mind to some; but it was the war that put suspicion in the minds of close friends and loved ones. Traitors in their midst made people very reluctant to express their views on any subject pertaining to war, in fear of what could happen to their families.

Usually about an hour before evening services started, several old men and women would lie in wagons and on benches, and their snoring sounded like growls; bears in the woods couldn't out-perform some of them.

Young girls would either be chased by boys or chase the boys, until things got out of hand. During church the children sometimes would try their hand at new sign language with facial expressions, indicating who liked the boy or girl next to them. When the giggling started, one could hear the sound of a hand across the side of a head, and the tittering would stop.

Christian love was often put to the test, especially toward families that had lost sons or relatives in battles at the beginning of the war. The families who were ostracized stayed to themselves and kept the pastor, Reverend Kelly, in much prayer.

The tradition of the church was that women were not allowed behind the pulpit, causing Mildred Watkins and other ladies to read scriptures from the pews. They gave some of the men bruised ankles when they started to nod.

When the Watkins returned home from church, Henry drove the wagon up close to the front porch, let the women out and drove the team on to the barn. He then unhitched the horses and turned them out to pasture.

Mildred entered the barn and approached Henry, saying, "We've had company."

"How do you know?" Henry asked.

"Come see. They left something on the porch. Two big sacks of something."

The two walked to the front porch. Violet was trying to open one of the sacks when Henry said, "Better be careful; something might jump out and bite you."

Paying no attention to her father's words, Violet said, "Feels like a lot of beans."

"Beans? Who in the world would leave a hundred-pound sack of beans on my porch?" Henry asked thoughtfully. He quickly unwrapped the wire that tied its top.

"Why, it's corn! Black corn! Well, I'll be," he said as he looked in both sacks.

Mildred looked on with amazement and declared, "Now who could have done such a thing, and what would anyone want with corn that has turned black?"

Henry quickly realized who had left the corn, and he knew what it was all about. He gently responded, "Honey, do you remember that fellow I told you about by the name of John Carter?"

Staring at the sack, Mildred nodded. Henry looked around for any sign of his friend. "He could have at least stuck around so I could thank him."

Violet took a hand full of corn and let it run through her little fingers and sift back into the sack.

"Stop that now. You and Gladys go change clothes and play somewhere. Your father will handle this, while I fix a bite to eat. Go on now, you hear!" Mildred snapped. Both girls scampered to their room to change clothes, while Henry threw one of the sacks over his shoulder and walked to the barn.

It was a beautiful spring day. The shining sun and the warmth of the air made people feel good. They were glad to be alive.

Eastern bluebirds were nesting in the little boxes Mildred had built and hung on the side of the large oak tree in the front yard. In the pasture the stock pond had a few wild geese that were late about leaving, swimming alongside some domestic ducks. They were looking for a last meal before making their departure.

Jonquils were in bloom, and across the meadow were wild flowers of different varieties that kept honeybees busy gathering nectar for their hives somewhere out in the forest.

About four hundred yards directly behind the Watkins' farm ran Miller Creek. This is where Henry's father built the Watkins Mill. It was built with a solid foundation of rock and very little wooden veneer, giving it the look of a painting. The force of the running stream turned the large paddle wheel. This turned the grinding stone during harvest, but it otherwise stayed raised until needed. This place served as one of the girls' secret places, when she wanted to be hard to find.

Mildred had their meal ready and went to the back porch and called her family, but only Henry came walking out the barn.

"Where are the girls?" Mildred asked.

"I don't know. I haven't seen them. I thought they were with you," responded Henry.

"Well, I sent them to the potato house over an hour ago. I thought they might be in the barn with you," she answered.

Greater Love Hath No Man

Henry walked to the potato house and sure enough, there they were in the loft, looking down. One of the girls called out, "Poppa, you better watch out! Old Billy is loose and he'll butt you!"

Henry saw the goat coming and quickly stepped to one side, grabbing the rope tied around Billy's neck. Henry threw him to the ground. "You can come down now. I've got him tied," Henry chuckled.

They walked to the house together; the girls carrying the potatoes. Gladys asked her father, "You gonna tell Mama that old Billy had us treed in the loft, Poppa?"

Looking down at her and smiling, Henry said, "Well, bright eyes, I suspect she already knows."

When they stepped up onto the back porch, Mildred met them at the door. "It took you two long enough. I was right before coming to find you," she scolded. They never said a word.

Henry poured water from a bucket into the wash bowl, and while the girls were washing their hands Gladys looked at her father and whispered, "Poppa you ain't gonna tell her, are you?"

With a big wink Henry said, "Why don't we sit down and eat our supper?"

Early the next morning, Violet went to her parents' bedroom door. Trying not to wake her father, she softly called out, "Mama." After a few seconds, she called out again a little louder, "Mama."

Mildred got out of bed quickly, leaving Henry sleeping. She knew something was wrong. "What's the matter?" She asked.

"It's Gladys! She's throwing up all over the place!"

Mildred lit a lamp, and holding it high, walked to the girls bedroom.

"Light another lamp and get a rag and a bucket of water; also stoke the embers in the stove and put some water on to boil."

Violet did as she was told while Mildred removed the bedding. Gladys had a high fever, and Mildred knew if she could wash the child's face with cold water first and then clean her with warm water, she stood a chance of getting the fever down. She knew Gladys was sick. Mildred hoped to let Henry sleep for a few more minutes, because at dawn he would be up and doing morning chores before breakfast.

Mildred washed Gladys and moved her to Violet's bed while she and Violet finished cleaning.

"We are through for now. Stay here and watch her while I go and wash up and get some coffee for your father," Mildred said.

"What if she starts vomiting again?" Violet asked.

"Then you put that bucket under her and let her do it in that, and come get me."

Violet was sitting on the end of the bed, nodding off to sleep when she heard her father speaking to her from the door way.

"What's going on?" Henry asked. It was dawn and the roosters were telling the world about it.

"Gladys is sick, Poppa. But Mama and me got her all fixed up for now," Violet said.

Henry walked over and put his hand on Gladys' forehead. "She has a fever. Where's your Mama?" Henry asked.

"She told me to stay here and watch Gladys, while she washed up and ground some coffee," she answered.

"Well, you do that, and I'll go see if I can help your mother, but come get us if it need be, you hear?"

"Yes, sir," she answered, looking at her sister worriedly.

Henry walked into the kitchen where Mildred was grinding coffee. "Do you think I should ride in and get Dr. Glass to come take a look at her?" Henry asked.

"Let's give it a little more time. Then, if I can't get the fever down, you should," Mildred answered.

"I'll feed and water the stock. Tell Violet to stay and help you with bright eyes," Henry said, walking out the back door.

Clouds forming in the east indicated that rain was coming, causing spring tilling to be postponed for a few more days. Henry didn't mind. This would allow him an opportunity to mend some harnesses and to shoe his big gray horse.

Walking back to the girls' bedroom, Mildred said, "Whew! Let's raise these windows and let some fresh air in!"

Gladys was awake, but still feverish, and Mildred was starting to worry. She turned to Violet and said, "Go tell your father to fetch Doc Glass. Hurry now!"

Violet ran out the back door shouting, "Poppa, come quick!"

Henry had already saddled up the big gray. When he heard Violet calling, he knew what must be done. Mounting the horse, he shouted back, "Tell your mother I've gone for Doc Glass!" And in a full gallop he rode out of sight, his expression showing his deep concern for his daughter.

Chapter seven

When Henry unsaddled his mount, both man and beast were drenched.

Spring rain was setting in bringing a slight chill with it. Meeting Henry at the door Mildred said, "If you don't get out of those wet clothes, Gladys won't be the only one sick".

"How is she," Henry asked?

"She's doing fine. Her fever broke about ten minutes after you left," Mildred responded.

"Has she eaten anything?" Henry asked.

"Little girls with the mumps just sip broth, for now," Mildred answered. "She's asking about you, but first get out of those wet clothes," Mildred replied.

Walking to the bedroom to do as she ask, Henry said, "Old Doc wasn't there so I left a note telling him to come quick as he can,"

"Well, Rosemary wasn't there, either?" Mildred asked.

"Like I said, no one was there." Henry replied. Quickly he changed clothes and walked barefooted to the living room and sat down in his favorite chair near the fire place.

Mildred brought him some dry socks and while he began putting them on, she knelt beside him laying her head next to his arm, and said, "Henry, I'm frightened."

With his other hand he began rubbing her cheek. Turning her face toward him, and bending down, he kissed her lips. "No need to worry I had the mumps when I was about her age and Thomas caught them from me and guess what? We both survived".

With tears, she looked deep into Henry's eyes saying, "It's not the girls that I'm so worried about, Elizabeth and I both had the mumps when we were girls, too. It's you that concerns me; it's us as a family that has me tangled up inside."

Lightning with drum rolls of thunder brought the rain down much harder. The sound of dogs barking alerted the Watkins they were about to have company. They waited for a knock on the door but a few minutes passed and still no knock.

"You don't have your boots on, I'll go," Mildred said in a low voice. Carrying a lamp with her she went to the door.

"You goanna let a body sit out here all night and drown," came a voice from a one horse drawn buggy. It was Rosemary. Henry knew the sound of her voice and quickly went to the bedroom and put his wet boots back on.

"You shouldn't come on a night like this," Mildred said.

"Nonsense, the note said come quick as I can, so here I am. Where's Gladys?" Rosemary asked. Holding the lamp high Mildred led her down the hall to the children's' bedroom.

Violet had a lamp lit and was reading to Gladys.

When Violet saw Rosemary, she jumped up and ran to her, hugging her around the waist crying, "Aunt Rosemary".

Henry took rosemary's horse and buggy to the barn. He knew they had a guest for the night. Walking back to where the women were and peeking through the doorway, he said, "Got some hot coffee on the stove."

When Gladys heard Henry's voice she began weeping, "Poppa, come close."

Bending down, smiling, he said, "Are you dying bright eyes"?

"Yes, Poppa, I'm a goner," she answered.

Rosemary butted in, saying, "Little girls don't stop kicking around here with mumps. It's just a little discomfort under their jaws for a while, you'll live".

"Did you hear that, Poppa, Aunt Rosemary said I'll live".

"Yeah, I heard, bright eyes," Henry replied. "Now you do what Aunt Rosemary and your momma tells you, while I go to the kitchen and pour the women folk some hot coffee, okay?"

"I wish i could drink coffee," Gladys said as Henry left the room. Later at the table rosemary complemented Mildred for diagnosing Gladys symptoms, saying, "You did right by trying to get her fever down, sometimes children can scare the daylights out of you when they get sick". The two women sat and talked while Henry went back into the sitting room to pull off his wet boots, again.

Setting them next to the fire place so they could dry out he walked back into the kitchen to join the women. Calmly, Rosemary said, " Mildred tells me you met my uncle and beautiful Caroline at Carter Town."

Sensing a touch of sarcasm, Henry hesitated before answering. "Yes, I did. They invited me into their home gave me a bath and fed me." Henry responded. "You didn't tell me about the bath," Mildred responded.

"Well I meant to, because I was pretty ripe about that time, and the river was up, and besides, it was cold." Henry said.

"Henry Watkins, is there anything else you've left out?" Mildred questioned.

"Now, now, honey that's all that's worth telling. I didn't think you would be interested in me taking a bath," Henry said.

"When it comes to beautiful women and you needing a bath, you bet I'm interested," Mildred spoke sharply.

Detecting a little jealousy, Henry said, "I took a bath in a private room and no body was in there but me, but I will admit that a well rounded fine lady gave me a hair trim though."

Rosemary watched the expressions on both their faces and with a short giggle she said, "Hey, you two, I didn't come here to start something, but I feel I must warn you, Henry, that my uncle is a southern loyalist and Caroline frequents the company of a person believed to be a northern spy by the name of Rose O'Neal Greenhow."

That name soared through Henry's brain like lightning. He thought, *That's the woman John had asked if I knew. I wonder what she has to do with Dr. Glass and his daughter?*

"Do you remember when we were girls in school and you had such a crush on Thomas and I liked the Lowery boy?" Mildred asked.

Rosemary snickered, "Yes, and Henry got mad and threw him in the creek. I thought the boy was going to drown before we could get him out." Henry never said a word.

"You were always plain spoken, Rosemary. Remember when the Jones boys were beatin' up on Joshua Kline and you took up for him?" Mildred asked.

"Yes, and I got sent home for that., Was my father ever furious!" Rosemary smiled.

"If I recall, you might not have gotten sent home if you hadn't told them you'd cock their hats for them. Un-lady-like! Yep, un-lady-like," Henry said walking back to the fire place to check on his boots.

It was getting late and the rain kept pouring down. Breaking up the conversation Mildred said, "Come, and I'll show you to your room if you're ready to turn in."

Rosemary yawned, and said, "I am a little tired. I think I'll take you up on that, but first I want to check on Gladys."

Both women walked to the children's bedroom just to find the two little ones were fast a sleep. While lightning a lamp in the guest bedroom Mildred ask with a serious tone in her voice, "Rosemary, do you think you and Thomas will ever marry"?

Before answering, rosemary hesitated. "We talked about it, but it's the war that has him not me," she replied.

Mildred didn't carry the conversation any further. "Well good night. I'll have Henry fetch your bag and put it by your door." Mildred said on the way out.

Mildred walked to the sitting room and found Henry once again near the fire place in his favorite chair. "You coming to bed?" she asked.

"I'll be along shortly," he answered.

"Oh, by the way would you mind getting Rosemary's bags out of the buggy?" she asked.

"They're in her room, over in the corner," Henry told her.

Patting Henry on the shoulder, she said, "Well, ain't you the smart one!"

When Henry did go to bed it seemed like he had just shut his eyes when he heard the dogs barking, again.

This time the company was wearing sabers that clang each step the horses took. The wet ponchos hid their identity making it hard for one to tell witch army they represented.

He heard sound of footsteps on the porch, and then bang, bang, bang. Someone was pounding on the door waking everyone in the house. Henry, in his long underwear, jumped out of bed, grabbed his Colt revolver and easing to the front window.

"Stay out of sight, and let me handle this," came a voice from the kitchen. It was Rosemary, and she was lightning a lamp. When she passed by the flour barrel she reached inside and pulled out a handful flower wiping it on her face. Henry watched in amazement.

Walking to the door and holding up the lamp close to her face she said, "Who are you men and what do you want?"

The man doing the pounding walked back to his horse and mounted while a voice said, "Ma'am, I'm Major Collins of the West Virginia Volunteers. I understand there are southern supporters living here, and I have orders to arrest everyone on the place."

"Major, I'm Rosemary Sewell Glass. My father is Doctor Glass of Mineral Wells, and I'm here trying to save the lives of the people that live here. As far as southern patriots, my dear Major, that couldn't be farther from the truth of any that occupy these premises. Besides, Major, if you or your men haven't been exposed to diphtheria, I would advise you to go from this place."

"Did you say diphtheria"?

"My dear Major, I'm not in habit of repeating myself, so if you and your men would kindly leave and let me get some sleep I would appreciate it". Rosemary could hear some of the men mumbling among themselves.

Major Collins knew his men were a bit jumpy over what she said, and not wanting to take the chance of it not being true, the Major humbly said, "Sorry to have troubled you, Miss Glass. Please give your father my regards, and by the way it might be a good idea if you get him to check you over. You're as pale as a ghost."

Rosemary walked back into the house as the horsemen rode away.

Mildred stood at the kitchen doorway with both girls peeking out around her.

Rosemary walked to the water bucket to wash the flour off her face. "Now, maybe we all can get some sleep around here she growled."

The aroma of eggs and bacon cooking on Mildred's stove drifted down the hall to the guest bedroom arousing its occupant.

It was daylight and Rosemary knew she had to get ready to leave. Pouring water from the picture into the bowl, she began washing her face when from beneath the covers on her bed came a whisper, "Aunt Rosemary, are you fixing to leave now?"

"You go back to sleep, and I'll come wake you before I do" Rosemary whispered back.

Walking down the hall to the kitchen, she met Mildred coming to check on the girls. "Last night seemed to have been a busy night for visitors, you'll find two more in my bed" Rosemary said.

"Figured that, there's hot coffee on the stove" Mildred said smiling

"Oh, let 'em sleep, lets have some coffee. I need to talk to you and Henry, anyway" Rosemary grumbled.

While the two women sat at the table talking, Henry came though the back door carrying a milk pale, saying, "Tell Violet she needs to start pulling that latch tighter. That calf got to its momma, and I only got a half a pale this morning."

Setting the pale down on the end of the table Henry walked to the stove and poured himself a cup of coffee. "Dang that's hot" Henry growled. Sitting down at the table, he stirred his coffee, while listening to the women chat about different things. Not a word was mentioned about the late night visitors.

When Rosemary went back to her room to finish dressing, Mildred said "Rosemary had two bed partners last night." Henry never uttered a sound but kept sipping his coffee.

After several minutes of silence Rosemary walked back into the kitchen. "I'm ready for some of those eggs and bacon, I seem to have both eyes open, now". All three began eating, not saying a word.

It was Henry that broke the silence, stating "Your buggy is ready. I pulled it around in front of the house."

"Are you trying to get rid of me, Henry?" Rosemary asked.

"Heck no, I just wanted you to know, that's all" Henry replied.

"If you two would excuse me, I think I need to go and make the girls get back in their bed," Mildred said.

When Mildred left the room, Rosemary said, "Now that she's gone, I want to talk to you".

"Fire away," Henry answered.

"When I get ready to leave, walk to the buggy with me. I'll speak to you there."

Mildred came back into the kitchen shaking her head saying, "Those girls are a handful, at times, a person wouldn't think that Gladys was ever sick".

Gathering up the dishes and putting them in a dish pan to wash, Rosemary said "Here, let me help you with those."

Mildred refused by saying, "There aren't that many, and besides, I know you are needed elsewhere. You don't know how much I appreciate you for coming. Henry, I put her bags in the hallway. Take them to her buggy, if you will," Mildred asked.

Rosemary knew that Mildred was worried, but remained silent. Walking to the front door she turned, putting her hands on her hips, trying to leave with a little humor she took a deep sigh, saying, "Well, if that's the way you feel."

Almost laughing out loud Mildred walked to where she was. Giving her a big hug and kissing her on the jaw, she said, "You know better than that".

"Just a little humor, precious, just a little humor," Rosemary answered, walking out the door.

"I'll see you off," Henry said walking out the door behind her. Henry put her bags in the buggy and before she drove away, she said "For what it's worth, Juba Baker, old man Tom Baker's boy, turned twenty last week, and is itching to join the army. A person might offer old man Tom three hundred dollars and let him go in his place."

"Nah, if the kid got killed out there, I could never forgive myself" Henry responded.

"Well, Henry, he's going, anyway. Soon, they'll get him in the draft, so why not?" Rosemary asked. "If its money, I've got the money. Mildred and the girls need you, but just think about it?" Rosemary asked again.

Henry never responded, but just watched her as she drove away.

Greater Love Hath No Man

Walking to the barn Henry pondered on what they talked about. Its planting season for some, but Henry had learned as a boy never to put a seed in the ground until after Easter. Virginia weather had a history of late frosts, and sometimes snow in April, but usually after Easter, chances of having to replant were very slim.

The Baker farm set off the main road east of Mineral Wells, and Rosemary had promised to look in on them the next time she was in the area. With Juba itching to go to war, she thought this might be a good time to visit. The road was sloppy and muddy causing her to drive slow. When she turned her horse off the main road onto the Baker road, her buggy slipped into a deep rut, banging against a sharp rock, and warping the wheel. Giving her horse a command of "Whoa!" the animal stopped.

She got out and walked up the muddy road, the Baker's old hound meeting her halfway. "Now, don't you get no stupid ideas, dog, about biting me, or it will be the last thing you ever do," she told it sternly.

The old hound must have known she carried a double shot derringer on her, because he trotted along beside her, wagging his tail every step of the way to the house.

The Baker men were all in the barn; it was the lady of the house, Mrs. Baker, that met her at the door.

"Look at you, Miss Rosemary, you're muddy as an old red eyed hog. Come in this house and lets get you washed up," she said. "I'm so glad to see you, I've been having this here terrible pain that runs up my back all the way to my head. Sometimes, I just don't think I'm going to make it" she said grunting.

"I left my bag in the buggy. If you'll send someone to fetch it, I'll give you something for that pain, but first let me wash up if you don't mind," Rosemary answered.

The Baker woman looked over at one of her girls who sat near the fire place cutting out paper dolls, and said,

"Go fetch your Paw and your brothers, and tell them that Dr. Rosemary is here".

The little girl dashed out the back door to the barn. "I'm not a doctor. I have had some training, but I'm not one, yet" Rosemary stated.

"Well you are to us," the Baker lady responded".

When Tom Baker came in the back door, his three sons followed. "Howdy, Doctor. What brings you out this way on such a muddy day?" he asked.

Before Rosemary could respond, old Tom growled to his wife, "Woman, fetch some coffee and pour Juba some, he's a man now."

"Mr. Baker, that's what I came to talk to you about is Juba, but first I wonder if you or one of your boys would go and help with my buggy. I seemed to have busted a wheel," Rosemary replied.

A hush came over the room before Tom spoke. "Juba, you and the boys go take the doctors' buggy to the barn". When the lads left the house old Tom asked, "What you want to talk about concerning Juba, Doc"?

When Mrs.. Baker brought the coffee Rosemary said, "You probably need to sit down and hear as well, because it will take the both of you to get it done if we agree."

The Bakers listened close as Rosemary began explaining about Henry's situation and how the Federals came to arrest him and his family. She also explained how the conscription act worked, and had the money with her to close the deal.

Tom Baker remained silent looking at his wife. "Now, let me get this right. Henry Watkins wants my boy to go in his place to fight in the war?" Tom asked.

Very sharply, Rosemary responded, "No, that's not right. Henry knows nothing about this and he wouldn't agree with it at all if he knew. It would have to be our secret and ours alone, but of course, Juba has to agree to it, as well".

Mrs. Baker spoke up, and said, "Doc, I don't want my boy going to no war, but it don't look like I can stop it."

"That no good brother of his that's fighting for the south – have our boys in blue killed him, yet" Tom asked?

Rosemary remained silent searching for wisdom to respond.

The youngest of the Baker's boy came in interrupting, saying "Paw, that wheel got busted up real bad, but Juba pulled the one off our old buggy and it fit, he's putting it on now".

"Tom, I'll pay you what ever you think is right for the wheel, and if we can come to some kind of agreement about what we've discussed, I'll pay you for that as well," Rosemary said.

Looking over again at his wife "What ye say, woman, he's gonna get drafted anyway, and this way he will have some money when he comes home." Tom said.

Mrs. Baker asked, "Doctor Rosemary, do you think this war will last much longer"?

Rosemary dropped her head, saying "Lord only knows, but for all our sakes, I hope it's over real soon."

Tom sent the boy to fetch Juba, but before he left, Rosemary asked him to bring in a bag that had a red ribbon tied around its handle. When they returned she open the bag and took pen and paper saying "Juba, I'm going to write a letter to whom it may concern pertaining to what your father and mother have agreed on, indicating that you are representing another person who has paid the necessary funds, is that all right with you?"

Studying the faces of his parents, all three signed making it legal. Reaching in the bag once more she pulled out a small drawstring purse and counted out three hundred dollars in Federal currency. "Now, Mr. Baker, what do I owe you for the wheel?" she asked.

Mrs. Baker interrupted, saying, "About as much as these pills are worth you gave me, Doc, ain't that right, Tom" she stated flatly.

Easter Sunday brought people from miles away who never came to church except for this day of year. Reverend Kelly was delighted, because there would be many events taking place. For the children, there would be sack races, a hopscotch contest, and then the Easter egg hunt. Finding the prize egg this year would be something different. The children could hardly wait.

Miller Creek ran about three hundred yards behind the little church, and usually that is where the tug of war game took place. This year would be different. Because water in the creek was high and swift, the deacons voted to dig a pit instead.

Henry was elected to do most of the digging. With so few young men left in the community, he chose two old men to help and did most of the digging himself.

Seeing Henry tackle the chore, Tom Baker came to help. Henry, knowing how Tom felt about him and Thomas, he was surprised.

"Looks like you could use a hand, I'll spell you," Tom said, reaching down and pulling Henry out of the pit. Henry smiled and handed him the spade.

Mildred was with a group of ladies showing off quilting patterns when Henry approached them.

Mrs. Baker said to Mildred, "I'll explain these new patterns to the ladies if you two want to be alone."

Mildred smiled and said, "Why thank you, Mrs. Baker; that is sweet of you. We'll just get some lemonade and be right back."

"Oh, no hurry. You just take your time," she replied.

Mildred and Henry sat at a long table and stared at each other. Mildred smiled and quietly said, "You know,

Reverend Kelly has always said the power of prayer changes things, and we have just witnessed a miracle."

"Look who's using my spade," nodded Henry.

"One of the ladies told me that the Baker's oldest boy left to join the West Virginia Cavalry last week. Maybe this is some kind of penance," Mildred whispered.

"Well, what ever it is, I like it," Henry answered.

The events were about to start. Children entering the sack race had begun to gather at the starting line. Violet and Gladys stood side-by-side, waiting for the word.

Reverend Kelly made sure everyone was ready and at the starting line.

"GO!" He shouted, and twelve children started jumping into sacks; they looked like a bunch of rabbits trying to get out of a snare.

When the last racer crossed the finish line, Reverend Kelly announced the winners.

Gladys finished in third place, and Violet finished fourth. When Gladys received her white ribbon, she ran to Mildred saying, "I would have gotten the blue one but Violet kept getting in my way."

When Henry noticed the men gathering around Reverend Kelly, he joined them. Reverend Kelly greeted him, saying, "Henry, I'd like for you to meet Dan Holland, from over near Carter Town."

Pausing for a moment, Henry reached and shook his hand, saying, "Watkins is the name. Nice meeting you."

"Watkins. I've heard that name before," Holland said.

Casually, Henry answered, "Yep, there's a few of us in these parts."

One of the older men interrupted the conversation. "It's time for the tug."

Reverend Kelly asked Henry to choose his team. As he was choosing, Tom Baker spoke up, "I'll be on Henry's side." When they realized there were only nineteen men total, Dan Holland asked to join, bringing the two sides to ten apiece.

Both sides dug their heels in to the earth, holding the big rope as tight as they could, waiting for Reverend Kelly to give the command.

"GO!" Reverend Kelly shouted and the tug commenced. Both teams grunted and growled furiously while the women stood on the sidelines and cheered.

Henry's team was gaining ground when, suddenly, some of the older men gave way, giving Holland's side the advantage. And pulling Henry and his teammates into the pit, head first.

Henry was exhausted. Tom Baker laughed and put his arm across Henry's shoulder. "Now that's what I would call fun."

As they helped one another out of the pit, Tom said, "Watkins, instead of me taking my crop into Mineral Wells this year, I think I'll bring it to you to grind for me, if you want to."

Taking a deep breath, Henry said, "Yep. I can use all the work I can get."

Glancing at the women, Henry made an excuse and went to speak to Mildred. Taking her hand, he said, "Come on, let's you and I walk down to the creek."

The path was long, narrow, and hidden from view by several large oaks trees. Henry bent down and gave Mildred a kiss. "What's that for?" she asked.

"That, my love, is because I'm alive, and I have the greatest woman in the world."

"Well, then, I'll let you do that, again," she replied.

Picking her up and bringing her close, Henry kissed her again.

An old woman coming back from the privy stopped and giggled saying, "Now you know people gonna talk."

Henry looked into Mildred's beautiful green eyes and said, "Let 'em."

Greater Love Hath No Man

When the old woman got about halfway up the path she turned and said, "They're getting ready for the egg hunt, you two."

Henry put Mildred down. With a grin, she said, "We better go be with the girls. We'll finish this tonight, at home."

All the children were gathered, waiting for the signal. The adults hid the eggs in tree trunks, hollow logs and even under the steps of the church. When the signal was given to start, children stampeded like cattle.

The prize egg had many colors and was found by one of the Baker girls. Everyone laughed when the prize was given. Her father had donated a six-week-old pig for the occasion. The little girl was delighted when she received her reward, because it was the same one she had pleaded with her father to let her keep.

When Reverend Kelly heard of the incident, he said, "God moves in mysterious ways."

As the day ended, people bid farewell and left for their destinations, leaving a few people behind to clean up the area and fill in the tug of war pit. Each year the Watkins family stayed, but this year the Watkins' had some help. Tom Baker said, "If I dug the thing, I should stay to fill it back in."

With a grin, Henry handed him a spade.

On the way home, Mildred rested her head on Henry's shoulder while a pair of Jenny mules pulled their wagon slowly down the road. The girls tried sleeping but the bumps from deep ruts kept them awake.

It was almost dark when the Watkins drove up to their front porch. "All right girls, wake up; we've got things to do," Mildred said softly.

Both girls climbed out the back of the wagon, as Violet said, "No sleeping back here. The road was too bumpy."

Henry drove the wagon to the barn while the women went inside. When he unhitched the team to let them out to pasture, he noticed a large knot on the leg of one of his mules. He ran his hand across the swollen leg. He was beginning to worry, so he decided to keep the injured mule in the corral over night and check on her the next morning.

Everyone was tired, and the last thing they wanted was supper. Mildred never had to order the girls to bed. They were asleep by the time their heads touched their pillows.

Whatever Mildred had in mind earlier that day would have to wait, too, because Henry began snoring the moment he shut his eyes.

The morning sun brought beams of light through their bed room window, showing dust particles floating in the air.

Henry had been up for an hour, working with the mule's leg in hope of getting the swelling down. Mildred wasn't aware of the horseman that rode up in their front yard. The horseman sat and waited patiently, never saying a word.

Gladys saw him first. She quickly ran to the kitchen, shouting, "Mama! There's a man out front sitting on his horse!"

As she wiped her hands on her apron, Mildred walked to the door, saying, "You girls stay inside while I see what the man wants."

Walking on the front porch she could see who it was. Mildred never gave him permission to get off his horse but spoke from where she stood. "What you want so early in the morning, mister?" she asked.

The horseman answered, "Is your man around, Mrs. Watkins?"

Greater Love Hath No Man

Mildred remembered meeting the man at the church social, but she was determined to find out his business before giving out any information.

"Your husband and I were in the tug of war event. I'm Dan Holland, from over Carter Town way. Remember?" he asked.

Mildred well remembered what Henry had told her about Carter Town and Thomas' situation. She wasn't about to tell him anything until he made himself plain. "Well Mr. Holland, what is it that you want?" she asked again.

Dan sensed her distrust and quickly responded, "Mrs. Watkins, I mean you or your family no harm. I'm on my way back home, and Reverend Kelly said I might want to stop by and say hello on the way."

Mildred was satisfied with his answer and told him Henry was in the barn. Dan never dismounted until reaching the barn. Walking quietly in the barn he could see Henry bending down, doctoring the mule's leg. Henry didn't notice his presence, until Dan spoke.

"Looks like a pulled tendon from here," Dan said.

Henry was startled. Trying to keep his composure, he replied, "Know a lot about doctoring mules?"

Dan walked over and rubbed the animal's leg. "Know that she's pulled a tendon and it'll be all right in a day or so, if you don't try working her."

"What brings you around so early?" Henry asked.

"That's the third time I've been asked that question this morning," Dan replied.

"Sorry, Dan, but the way things are these days, it keeps a body kind of touchy," Henry responded.

"Man, I'm just passing through and was asked to bring you a message from a fellow that left something on your porch not long ago."

Patting the mule on the neck and walking around so he could look Dan in the eyes, Henry asked, "How is John these days?"

Making eye contact with Henry, Dan answered, "He's well, and Carter Town is being rebuilt slowly. He also asked me to try to get you to come back with me for a few days. Something to do with your brother, Thomas."

Henry walked over to a door that opened to the corral. Turning the mule out, he turned and said, "Dan, have you had your coffee yet?"

Watching every move Henry made and hesitating before responding, Dan shook his head.

"Let's go inside. I believe the wife should have some on the stove," Henry said.

The men walked to the house, meeting Mildred on the back porch. "I see you found him, Mr. Holland," Mildred said and smiled.

She knew something was up, but she would just have to wait to find out. The two men sat at the kitchen table sipping hot coffee. Violet came in and sat by her father. "Where's your sister?" Henry asked.

"In her room, reading," she answered.

"This is my daughter, Violet," Henry introduced. "Go get your sister," Henry said.

After cleaning the back porch, Mildred walked to the stove, poured a cup of coffee and sat next to Henry. She just listened to the two men talk. Gladys came in and stood beside her father. "This is Gladys; my other daughter, Dan," Henry introduced.

Dan smiled at both girls and said, "Glad to know you, ladies."

Mildred waited for his real reason for this visit to surface. Sending the girls off to their rooms, Mildred asked Dan how long he had known Reverend Kelly.

"He's my mother's brother," he answered.

"So, he's your uncle," Mildred replied.

Greater Love Hath No Man

Nodding and sipping his coffee, Dan responded, "Yes." Henry sensed Mildred's suspicion. Looking at Mildred, Henry lowered his voice and said, "It's Thomas."

Without a word, she walked to their bedroom and prepared his bed roll. Dan walked outside and stood next to the porch, lighting his pipe while the couple talked things over.

All the time Mildred was packing his bed roll she never said a word. Henry stood at the bedroom door watching. When she finished, she handed it to him.

Dropping it to the floor, Henry picked her up and kissed her.

"There are two in there that's going to want to know what's happening. Are you going to tell them, or do I get stuck with the job again?" Mildred questioned.

Ignoring her question, Henry put Mildred down and picked up his bed roll. Walking to the back door, Henry said "If for some reason something should happen to me, I want you and the girls to go to Rosemary's."

"Something is not right about this, Henry," Mildred insisted.

"Yep, I feel it too; but what if Thomas does need me, then what?"

With tears running down her cheeks, she cried, "Then go and get your self killed! See if we care!" Walking out the door, Mildred ran to his side, crying, "I didn't mean it. God knows I didn't mean it."

Henry turned and kissed her again. "Remember, if I don't make it back, go to Rosemary's. Promise me, you hear!" Henry demanded.

Wiping tears from her eyes, she nodded her head. She and the girls watched as the men rode out of sight.

Chapter eight

The two men rode a steady pace with the sound of leather stretching with each step their horses made. Motioning for Henry to stop, Dan dismounted and tightened the cinch on his saddle.

Henry dismounted and walked to some bushes to relieve himself. "Which way did you come when you left Carter Town; down the pike or through one of the back trails?" Henry asked.

"Came down the logging trail behind Butcher's tavern. Just too many deserters along the pike," Dan answered.

Henry nodded his head in agreement. From where they were, Henry knew a shortcut to the tavern but it would take them through Butchers hollow, the same place he had helped the Confederates just weeks before.

With Dan agreeing, both horsemen rode down the slope into the hollow. Looking across an opening, Dan spotted wood smoke hovering over the treetops. "Hold up a minute, Watkins; we've got company up ahead."

Henry looked the direction in which Dan was pointing and noted, "From the looks of all that smoke, I'd say there are several camp sites, wouldn't you?"

There was no choice! They could take their chances, riding by in hope of not being seen or turn around and take the pike.

Henry spotted a deer trail that ran along the edge of the hollow to the forest. If they could make it to the woods without being seen, they would have a chance. "What do you think?" Henry asked.

"Lead the way" Dan responded.

Henry dismounted and walked with his hand over the nostrils of his horse. Henry began the task of easing along the trail. Loose rocks would roll, clanging against one another, causing Henry to stop quite often. Dan followed behind him, walking his horse.

They came to a small opening where they could be seen. Henry paused before crossing. He could see a Federal picket guard from where he stood.

Using sign language and pointing to Dan, Henry motioned when the guard turned his back to them so they could cross. It would be fifty yards of breath taking steps but in the forest it was Butcher's tavern all the way.

Slowly, walking his mount and watching the guard, Henry made it across. Concealed from the guard, Henry motioned for Dan to come across. Just as Dan started, the guard turned and looked in his direction. Dan froze, waiting.

The sentry turned and began talking to another guard, without seeing Dan. When he reached Henry, Dan was white as a ghost. He whispered to Henry, "Either that guard was blind or just don't give a damn. He looked straight at me, turned, and started talking to another guard. Neither one of them saw me."

"He probably had smoke in his eyes. We better get on if we're going to make Bertha's by dark," Henry said.

The deer trail ended at Cub Run. Henry knew the creek ran behind Butcher's Inn. He had crossed it several times. There was an hour of daylight left when they reached the back of the inn.

Henry watched for any movement, but there was none. He listened for voices and the sound of music, but all was quiet. Too quiet.

"Something ain't right at Bertha's. It's not like her place to be quiet. There ain't even a chicken walking around," Henry said.

"Let's leave our horses here and walk over there to see what's going on," Henry suggested. Dan nodded in agreement. Both men quietly approached the back of the barn. Henry walked around the barn on one side, while Dan took the other, meeting each other in the front. Henry could hear blow flies buzzing. The barn door was wide open, and nothing stirred. Henry knew something was wrong when old Nigger Sam wasn't singing or moving around close.

Dan eased closer and asked, "What do you think?" Both men drew side arms and walked inside the barn. Henry quickly found why the blow flies were there. The body of old Nigger Sam was hanging from a rafter.

"Now, who would want to go and do that to poor old Sam? He never hurt nobody," Henry said softly. Dan walked to the back door of the tavern and slowly walked inside.

Greater Love Hath No Man

The first room was empty, except for the body of Bertha Butcher lying in a pool of blood with her head split open by a double-bladed axe that lay near the front door.

Dan walked causally through the empty rooms and into the kitchen. There lay the bodies of two Negro women who had both been shot through the head.

When Dan returned to the barn, he found Henry had cut old Sam down. "Bertha and her two nigger cooks are dead, too," Dan said.

Looking at Sam lying on the ground, Henry said, "Who in the world would want to do a thing like this?"

Dan looked at Henry and said, "War Henry. It's war."

"Help me find a shovel. I'm going to dig old Sam a grave," Henry said.

"Well, we better dig three more for those inside don't you think?" Dan asked.

While the men were looking around for a shovel, they heard the sound of a wagon jostling down the pike. "He's turning off and coming this way. Maybe he'll give us a hand burying these folks," Henry said.

"No, lets get our asses out of here before we get blamed for all this," Dan argued.

Henry thought for a moment. "Yep, I think you're right."

It was dusk when they made it to their horses. "I bet that peddler thinks he's getting a room for the night, but he's gonna get something he'll tell his grandchildren about," Dan said.

"Yep. But don't think I would ever want to tell mine about it," Henry answered.

The sky was overcast, making it a dark night. They decided to make camp where they were. They had a perfect view of the tavern. They watched who ever was inside light several lamps.

Henry was almost asleep when he thought he heard a baby cry. "Did you hear a baby?" He asked.

"Yeah. Those folks down there have a baby with 'em," Dan answered.

Henry watched as lamps moved from place to place until he drifted off to sleep.

When morning came Henry was awakened by the smell of boiling coffee. "You were cutting logs over there. Didn't want to wake you," Dan greeted him.

"Yep. Been doing that too much here lately, according to the wife," Henry answered.

"Bunch of folks down there. Some more wagons came in just a few minutes ago," Dan said.

As he poured coffee, Henry said, "You know, something don't add up. We find old Sam and the women dead, no live stock any where around, and the place robbed of everything. Looks to me like they had been dead a long time, too, and Bertha has always had people there."

"Think about it, Watkins. Looks to me like a bunch of deserters came by and did 'em in and took everything in sight. I'm sure we weren't the first ones to leave them there," Dan answered.

"Maybe not," Henry responded. Slowly sipping his coffee, Henry asked, "Do you know my brother, Thomas?"

Dan ignored his question and walked over to the fire without answering. "Dan, I've been thinking about this trip. Maybe I need to head back home. I'm already late in planting."

Dan remained silent. Henry walked to his mount and without another word, began saddling his big gray.

Dan Holland finally responded, "He's wounded, Henry." Those words cut through Henry like a double edged sword.

Standing beside his mount and leaning forward, Henry put his forehead next to his saddle with his hand squeezing the saddle horn. "How bad is it?" He finally managed.

"I'm not sure. All I know is that John Carter said they had taken one of his boys and him to Maw Carter's place," Dan answered.

Henry mounted and said, "We're wasting time." Henry led the way, riding his gray harder than usual.

"Hey, Watkins, slow down some! No sense in killing our horses!" Dan shouted.

When they reached the outskirts of Carter Town, they could hear music with banjoes and fiddles, backed by harmonicas and Jews harps.

"Sounds like a shindig of some kind," Henry said. There, in front of Maw Carter's home was a company of Confederate cavalrymen.

The smell of barbeque got Dan's attention, "Smell that?" Dan asked.

Lying in a hammock, stretched between two oaks lay Thomas, snoozing like a baby. John Carter noticed the two riding up and walked out to greet them. "Well, you did come. Glad to see you, again," John said and smiled.

"Where's he at?" Henry asked rudely.

"Come on, Watkins, lets get some vittles," Dan said.

Ignoring Henry's rude behavior, John pointed toward the hammock. Henry walked to where Thomas lay, as John Carter followed. Dan headed straight to the table. Looking down at Thomas, John whispered, "Old Doc Glass got two chunks of lead out of his side, but he's tough. He'll make it."

While staring down at Thomas, Henry responded, "Dan said one of your boys got it, too. How's he doing?"

"Sitting over there bigger than you please, eating like he's starving to death," John replied.

"What say we let Thomas snooze, while we get something to eat. Ever eat any barbequed goat?" John asked.

As the two men walked toward the table Henry answered, "No, but I sure have been tempted a few times, back home."

"I think you'll like it. I killed and cleaned it myself. Maw has been fixing on the thing since daylight," John said.

Remembering the first time he had met John's mother, Henry commented, "Quite a lady, your Maw. Yep, quite a lady."

The table consisted of two long boards lying across several molasses barrels with one of Maw Carter's bed sheets as a tablecloth. It served the purpose.

Dan Holland sat next to Eli Carter. Eli talked about how he and Thomas came to be wounded.

Sitting down next to Dan, Henry said, "Maybe I should get in on this conversation."

Everything became quiet as Henry sensed an attitude toward him.

Sitting next to Henry, John Carter spoke, "Don't stop now, son, go on and finish your story."

Eli looked at his father and lowered his head. "Not much left to tell, Paw."

"Oh, go on son. You're in good company. Henry has never heard it before. Have you Henry?"

Henry never answered but sat quietly, eating. It was obvious that something was coming between John and his son and what ever it was, he didn't want to be involved.

With a dry stern voice John Carter said, "Let me say something here in front of all of you that sit at my table. No matter what you think of Henry Watkins, I invited him here, and he is as welcome in my home as any of you are! Is that understood?"

Silence was golden for the duration of the meal. Henry knew where he stood now, with this group. "Sorry about all this, Henry," John said.

"Hell, John, I go through this every Sunday at church. Ain't nothin' new," Henry responded.

He walked to his brother's hammock and stood, shaking his head. "Now look at you," he whispered, "all shot up and probably just as stubborn as always."

Remembering how close they had been when they were young made Henry smile.

"Remember the time I was courting Mildred, and you came over to see Elizabeth? The Davis boy was there with the same thing on his mind. Your old hunting hound sure messed things up for awhile."

Thomas opened his eyes and said, "Yeah, and how was I to know that old Blue was killing old man Adams' pigs that day?"

Thomas reached up for Henry to help him out of the hammock. "What brought you here? I know. I know. That big gray horse," Thomas chuckled.

John Carter approached, saying, "Well the dead has come alive."

Henry helped Thomas to a chair while John walked beside them. "Don't take John serious, Henry. He's always cracking jokes of some kind."

"Who's jokin'?" John asked. "The boys don't mean to be ornery. The way things seem, Henry, they're a little sore at you for not joining when they voted to accept you. That's all."

"Well the boys can get rid of their soreness," Thomas remarked.

"What happened? How come you and Eli got shot?" Henry asked.

"Had it not been for Mosby and his partisan rangers, we would all be pushing up daisies by now," Thomas said.

"Who's Mosby?" Henry asked.

John Carter answered, "Some of the Yankees call him the Gray Fox. Just like Simmons and his friends are calling your brother the sly one."

"Simmons? Why, Simmons is dead, ain't he?" Henry asked.

John Carter and Thomas stared at each other while Thomas said, "Not hardly."

"What happened after you guys left me and John that day?" Henry asked.

"Well, it's a long story, and I don't feel like talking about it right now. Some other time, perhaps," Thomas replied.

Realizing that Simmons would be another wound to Thomas' side, Henry decided to change the subject.

John Carter left the two brothers and walked back to the table to sit next to Eli. "You still eating?" John asked.

"Naw. Just thinking. Guess we've been pretty hard on old Henry. Can't blame a fellow much. If I had a wife and two kids, I'm not sure just what I would do, either," Eli answered.

Some of the men were gathering around Thomas paying their respects with, "Good to see you up and feeling better, Major."

"Major? Well, when did this happen?" Henry asked.

"Oh, about a week after we kicked Simmons' ass," Thomas answered.

"Simmons, again. Can't seem to do away with that name today for some reason," Henry noted.

A couple of the men started picking on their banjoes while some of the others joined in with a fiddle and a few Jews harps. It wasn't long before they were all sitting around Thomas and Henry picking and singing old church hymns.

"What yew wanna hear, Henry?" came a voice from the group.

"Y'all know 'Amazing Grace'?" Henry asked.

Greater Love Hath No Man

John Carter said, "Lets all sing it! Whady'all say?"

Folks who were trying to build back the town dropped their tools and walked to where the music was playing. Rebuilding Carter Town would just have to be put on hold for a little while longer.

A carriage drawn by two beautiful white horses and driven by a well-dressed light-skinned Negro man stopped near the crowd.

The driver got down and opened the door, assisting a young lady who was dressed in a blue, full-length dress and carried a blue parasol. Her white gloves were like snowflakes. It was Miss Caroline. Bonner held her hand as he walked her to where Thomas sat.

"Miss Caroline," Henry said.

"Why, Mr. Watkins, it's such a pleasure to see you again. How is your family?" She asked.

"They're fine, ma'am. Thank you for asking." Henry answered.

She walked to Thomas and kissed his cheek lightly. "How are you feeling today?" she asked politely.

Thomas took her hand and gave it a squeeze. "Better, thank you," he said and smiled.

By watching the two of them, Henry knew there was something more than just a causal visit.

John, obviously knowing more than he revealed, said, "Fellows, what say we all go over and sit under that clump of oaks and let the good doctor's daughter and the Major talk in private."

Henry walked away with the others, never looking back.

"Think he knows?" Caroline questioned Thomas.

"He knows," Thomas replied.

"I like him," she responded.

"I think there is something you should know before we start making any plans for the future," Thomas said.

"What? That you and my cousin Rosemary were seeing each other at one time?" she said and smiled.

Placing her hand on Thomas' shoulder she said "Well, my dear sweet Yankee cousin will just have to get over it."

Thomas patted her hand. "Things have a way of working out if you give it enough time, I suppose," Thomas whispered.

The men were gathered and playing music.

A dispatch rider approached Thomas and Caroline,. Politely removing his hat and bowing to Caroline, "Ma'am."

Turning his attention to Thomas, he handed a letter to the officer. "Begging the Major's pardon, sir, but headquarters wants a reply as soon as possible."

"Soldier, there's food and drink on that table over there. Help yourself while I prepare an answer."

The music had stopped the moment the dispatch rider rode in. The crowd was hushed, as they looked at Thomas. Henry noticed Caroline beckoning him to come.

Walking up to her, she said, "Help Thomas into the house where he can be alone for awhile."

Calling for Bonner, Caroline walked to her carriage. The men sat patiently, mumbling to one another.

Henry walked out of the house to where John Carter sat.

"Dan tells me that y'all ran into a bunch of Federals camped over in Butcher's holler," John said.

"Yep. Did he also tell you what we found at Bertha's place?" Henry asked.

John nodded his head and said, "Just a matter of time with old Bertha. Too bad about old nigger Sam, though. He was a good nigger; not too many like old Sam," John remarked.

The conversation ended as the two men watched Caroline get in the carriage. "Now, that's quite a lady.

Greater Love Hath No Man

Don't be surprised if she becomes your sister-in-law after this war is over," John remarked.

Henry never said a word but watched as Caroline's carriage rode out of sight. "John, I've got a question for you. That lady you asked me about named Rose... Why should I know her, and who is she anyway?"

John hesitated for a moment before answering, "I think your brother needs to tell you about that."

Henry and the men watched as the dispatch rider finished his meal and walked into the house.

One of the men began strumming his banjo and humming the tune of "Dixie".

Shortly, the rest joined in humming with him, standing at attention with their hats removed.

Henry watched the dispatch rider come out of the house and mount his horse. "Well, John, I think I'll see about the Major before I leave out of here."

"You leaving now, Henry?" John asked.

"Yep. April has slipped away and the May Pole is staring me in the face. Besides, I'm behind on my work. I'll be planting by lantern light if I don't get home soon. Oh, by the way, I want to thank you for the black seed corn. How come you didn't stick around for a good hot meal and meet the family, while you were there?" Henry asked.

"Sent it by Dan; he was going that way, anyway. Thought you might want to try your hand at raising some of that purple corn meal," John answered.

Thomas came out of the house and stood on the front porch, leaning against one of the main pillars. One of his soldiers who wore sergeant's stripes shouted, "Gather round men. The Major has something to say."

Thomas spoke with authority, "Fellows, there's a fight brewing. Hooker's boys crossed the Rappahannock above Fredericksburg. They are now probably close to Chancellorsville. We have been asked to assist our forces over on the Orange turnpike.

Shouting with a yell that would make a persons' skin crawl, the men rallied behind their commander. Henry was amazed at their loyalty. Henry knew not to say anything. Thomas would lead his men as long as he could sit a saddle.

In less than ten minutes a cloud of dust could be seen, as Thomas and his men rode out of sight.

Walking up to Henry, John said, "That's all he knows, Henry; let him ride out his destiny with pride."

"Humph! Pride? Is that what you call it? Reverend Kelly says that the Bible states pride comes before a fall." Walking to his big gray, Henry stopped and looked down the dusty road one more time.

Like a prayer, he whispered, "Farewell, my brother, farewell."

Greater Love Hath No Man

Chapter nine

Henry knew he had at least a full day's journey from Carter Town. Now he had to decide which way to go. He knew better than to go through Butcher's Hollow or to stop anywhere near Bertha's place, after what happened to her and the hired help. The last thing he needed was to run across a conscription broker from either side. This meant his best option would be to ride all night, taking the pike, rather than trying to camp along the timberline somewhere in between.

With the weather clear and a full moon on the rise, Henry began his long ride toward home.

The warm spring air felt good to his face as the big gray gracefully picked her pace along the winding dirt road. As he rode quietly, thinking of his family, Henry could smell honeysuckle and knew this fragrance would travel with him for miles.

With his hand near his revolver, he was prepared for anything... or so he thought. As he approached the first wide turn on the pike, a deer running across the road startled Henry and his horse. He settled the big gray mare by gently patting her neck and saying, "Easy, girl, easy."

Henry knew something had to scare the deer. He dismounted and stood quietly with his rifle at the ready. His horse could sense strange animals, and she still snorted and pranced around.

"Probably just a bear," he told his horse quietly, as he looked all around for any sign of movement. "Whatever it was, it's long gone by now," he said as much for his own good. He stood for a few more minutes before mounting up and riding on, still a little shaky on his insides.

As he rode the pike, his thoughts again turned to home and to his home state of Virginia. He thought about the tall trees and beautiful wildflowers of spring, high waterfalls and cool, clear streams. Henry was very proud to be a Virginian and often spoke of how wise he thought his parents were by keeping what his grandparents had established.

During the winter and rainy seasons, freight wagons had left deep ruts that hardened like rocks, causing Henry to ride the timberline at times. It was at one of these times that would change his life forever.

As Henry rode west toward Mineral Wells, with the moon just beginning to rise, he started to think how wise his decision was to ride at night, so the setting sun wouldn't blind him. As he rode over a small knoll, he came face-to-face with a Federal cavalry patrol. It was useless to try to outrun them.

Stopping his mount, he took a deep breath and sighed as he awaited his capture.

A young officer and a harsh talking sergeant approached him. Assuming Henry was a deserter, the young officer began asking him questions, while the sergeant rode around to the rear of Henry, blocking him from any escape attempt he might think about trying.

Thoughts of that nature were far from Henry's mind. He was no fool. He knew these men would shoot him if he made the slightest mistake.

Henry explained that he was just a farmer who lived near Mineral Wells, and he had been to see a sick friend. He told them that he was now on his way back home. Henry's age never entered the young officers mind until two men dressed in civilian clothes rode out of the column and approached Henry.

"How old are you, boy, and how come you're not in uniform?" one of the men asked. Henry didn't answer. Looking at the sergeant and smiling, the man said, "Looks like this one is hard of hearing."

"Thirty-five," Henry answered quietly.

"You have a reason for not being in uniform?" the officer asked?

"Yes. I'm a farmer and have a wife and two children," Henry answered.

"So is half my troop, but they're not afraid to fight for their country!" the officer declared.

"You got it wrong, mister. I'm not afraid to fight for my country. It's just that I have no intentions of fighting my country," Henry said, defiantly.

When the sergeant heard Henry's words, he struck him on the back of the head, knocking him to the ground.

Speaking to the men dressed in civilian clothes the officer said, "You two, pick him up and put him in the ambulance wagon. We'll settle this at headquarters."

Greater Love Hath No Man

    The moon was high in the sky when Henry came to his senses. Jostling around in the back of a wagon wasn't the easiest thing he had done all day. His head was throbbing as he reached up and rubbed where he had been hit. Blood was still oozing out of a small hole in his scalp. Looking out the back he could see his gray following, tied to the tailgate. Henry's thoughts of his family and the things he told Mildred were the only things on his mind. The lack of confidence in his future depressed him to tears.

    He managed to turn to a position that allowed him to see the back of the driver, but the handcuffs that secured him kept him from doing anything more. As he looked out the back of the wagon to watch his horse, he noticed the position of the still rising moon. He thought, we're traveling east, not west toward Mineral Wells.

    Occasionally, the driver would look back to check on Henry. One of the men dressed in civilian clothes rode up to the wagon and asked the driver how the prisoner was doing. Spitting out a mouth full of tobacco juice, the driver replied, "He's still back there, if that's what you're asking."

    The fullness of the moon was bright, as though it was a false dawn. Visibility was good.

    "Whoa!" yelled the driver, as he brought the wagon to a stop. The pike was narrow in places, making it difficult to pass.

    An old man with a long white beard pulled his wagon over. Waving his hat as he passed, he shouted, "Give those Johnnie Rebs hell for me, boys." As the ambulance wagon passed, the old man could see Henry sitting in the back.

    A short while later, the ambulance pulled off the pike into an opening where the troops had stopped for breakfast.

    Henry smelled wood smoke. The driver got down and walked to where troops were gathered, drinking coffee. Henry could hear them laughing and talking.

The driver returned to his wagon, untied Henry's horse, and moved her to a wheel by tying the reins there.

"Figure you need to get out and stretch your legs a mite and go piss or something," the man said to Henry. Henry was glad to hear those words, and he slid out the back. The driver unlocked the shackles, escorted him to a nearby tree, and waited while Henry relieved himself.

When he finished, they walked back to the wagon. "Bet you're hungry," the driver said, quietly.

"Yep, but I'd settle for a cup of that good-smelling coffee for now," Henry answered.

The driver put the shackles around Henry's ankles and locked them tightly.

"Loosen them a little, if you don't mind. They're about to cut off the blood," Henry said.

The driver bent down and released them some. "Now I'll get us some of that hot coffee, while you crawl your ass back up in that wagon," the driver said. Henry did as he was told.

He waited patiently, shutting his eyes and drifting in and out of short naps. The driver finally handed Henry a tin cup filled with coffee and said, "Here you go. Watch now, it's hot!"

"Got some beef jerky in my saddle bags if you care to fetch it," Henry said. The driver never paid any attention. Politely, Henry asked, "Ever eat any barbequed goat?"

That got the drivers attention. "What did you say?" he asked.

Henry repeated his question. "Hell no! I ain't about to eat no damn goat!" he responded.

"Well, you can have the beef jerky, and I'll eat the goat, if you get it out of my saddle bags," Henry offered.

Unwrapping both bundles, the driver asked, "Which is which?"

Reaching for the beef, Henry said, "The other one is the beef. You'll like the way my wife makes it. She fixes it with a barbeque flavor, sometimes."

Not knowing the difference, the driver chewed into the goat. "Sure in hell beats hard tack and salt pork," he commented.

Henry had planned to take the goat meat home to Mildred and the girls but watching the driver eat his words was much more satisfying.

After their meal, the driver growled, "We'll be pulling out soon, so I'm going over there by that tree to get some sleep, and if you plan on doing the same, you better get it done, now, because we got several more miles ahead of us."

"Where they taking me? Do you know?" Henry asked.

"Probably gonna send you to prison, but we're headed to Fairfax for now."

After a few hours, the troop was on the move again, with Henry still jostling around in the back of the ambulance wagon.

Meanwhile, the old man they had passed earlier was hurrying to his home. Seeing Henry in the wagon kept bothering him until he remembered where he had seen him before. He quickly drove his team off the pike and onto a trail that led to Carter Town. Stopping outside Maw Carter's home, he got down and walked to her door. Knocking several times and calling her name, he soon realized there was no one home. *Must be in town working on repairs*, he thought.

The old man climbed back up on his wagon, and was starting to drive off, when Maw came walking out of the garden. He saw her as she walked up to the wagon.

"Mr. Rivercomb, what can I do fer yew?" She asked.

"Is your son John around?" he asked.

"Gone to get one of my grandsons. He got shot up pretty bad over on the Orange the other day, whipping those blasted Yankees."

"I heard Gen. Lee put the hurt on those Bluebellies at Chancellorsville the other day. Was they in on that fight?" He asked.

"Don't rightly know, but John should be back in a day or so. Want me to tell him you need to see him about something?" She asked.

"Yeah, tell him that I passed a bunch of Yankees on the pike. They had a fellow shackled in the back of an ambulance wagon. He looked like that big man that come up to the cemetery looking for John. He was riding that gray mare the day we buried some of the town folk."

"You mean Major Watkins' brother?" she asked.

"I never got to meet the man. I saw him at a distance that day, but I'd know that big gray mare anywhere, and I bet money that's him."

"How did you get close enough to tell?" Maw asked.

"Made out like I was on their side. I was a cheering them on; drove the wagon so close, I thought our hubs would rub together. Best I be getting on home before dark. Just thought John should know."

"I'll tell him when he gets here, Mr. Rivercomb, and thank you for coming by," she replied.

Greater Love Hath No Man

Chapter ten

The Federal column that transported Henry reached a crossroad that intersected the main road into Fairfax and the town of Caldwell. In this area were several farms that harbored Confederate guerrilla fighters. It was here that the Yankees had set many traps to catch Thomas and his troops, failing in every attempt.

John Carter and Dan Holland had traveled this same road just hours before, bringing John's wounded son home.

The four-hundred acres the Davenport family worked near an old creek bed was impossible to see from the crossroads. Whenever the Federal columns rode near, one of the Davenport children would climb a tree and call down to their father to inform him of every movement the troops made. Old man Davenport was blind in one eye, but it never kept him from doing his work as a farmer.

In his old age he had managed to father three boys who worked better than two grown men, plus they could shoot a rifle better than most folks around there. He had other grown children who managed to raise families of their own; they all lived near each other.

People who knew the Davenports sometimes referred to Mrs. Davenport as "the old woman who lived in a shoe." Before the war, one of the standing jokes that circulated among the people who lived nearby was, "Jeff Davis needed not to gather up a vast army, just send the Davenports up to Washington and they would clean out the whole mess."

Federal troops were always searching for Thomas, but the Davenports developed a warning signal, which would alert each family, no matter the weather. Someone would always send the warning by blowing an old hollowed out cow horn. The women folks blew the thing better than most men did.

The moment the Federal column that was transporting Henry came past the first Davenport farms, every one in the valley knew. It was a four-mile stretch from the first farm to the last, and the column had to pass each one. The column would have to cross a dried creek bed, which ran from beside the old man's farm to past the last Davenport's place.

When the Federals reached a half way point they encountered a broken down wagon, full of hay and two of the Davenport women attempting to make repairs. The road was narrow; it would be very difficult to pass. The young officer sent the two conscription brokers to help move the wagon off the road. The women had unhitched the mules from the wagon, tying them to a nearby bush.

One of the men walked to the mules and reached to untie them, but he was surprised by a whisper from just behind the bush accompanied by the sound of a pistol being cocked. "Call your friend and be quick about it, or I'll blow the top of your head off."

The man did as was told as the troops sat, looking around for a possible ambush. The two women vanished into the woods. Once they were out of harms way, all hell broke loose.

The conscription brokers were the first to meet their Maker, followed by the young officer and several troopers. It happened so fast that the sergeant and the rest of the men threw down their firearms and surrendered.

"Yee-haw!" someone yelled, and Henry thought he recognized the voice.

The driver of the ambulance wagon surrendered peacefully and was soon gathered up with the rest, which left Henry still shackled.

One of the Davenport boys looked into the wagon and shouted, "There's a big fellow in here with chains on, Paw!"

One of the men walked to the back of the ambulance and looked in. "Well, I'll be! Fancy meeting you here!"

Henry's eyes lit up like a Christmas tree when he saw Dan Holland. "Man! Am I glad to see you! I thought I recognized that yell," laughed Henry relieved.

"Yeah, and I thought I recognized that big gray, but I wasn't sure," Dan answered.

Looking at the young Davenport boy, Dan said, "Go fetch the key off the driver, and lets get these things off this fellow. Soon as we get you loose Henry, we'll mosey up to the house and get a bite to eat. Besides, John and his boy Eli is up there, and they'll want to see you, again."

The shackles were off in less than a minute, and Henry untied his mount from the wagon and walked her to

Greater Love Hath No Man

the house with Dan. "Don't think Eli is gonna make it this time, Henry," Dan said.

"That's too bad. What happened?" Henry asked.

"Well, you know he got hit the same time Thomas got it, several days ago. Both of them should have stayed at Carter Town, but you know how your brother can get pig-headed at times. Well, Eli was the first one to get it again in this last fight up on the Orange. Things are different this time. It's bad, real bad," Dan answered.

Henry braced himself, expecting to hear about Thomas next. "My brother, Thomas. What about him?" Henry asked.

"I'll let John tell you about that," Dan replied.

"No, damn it! You're gonna tell me right now, before I go another step with you!" Henry shouted.

"He's alive, if that's what's bothering you, but they got him and three of his men as prisoners, and where they have taken them, God only knows," Dan said, quietly.

Henry stopped, and staring at Dan said, "Well, we'll just be finding out where he is then."

The ambush party gathered up all the spoils, taking the ambulance and the prisoners to one of the barns, hiding them inside. Horses and mules that were confiscated were taken to the old man's farm and turned loose in his pasture. The dead were stripped of everything, including their uniforms which the women washed and stored away.

The Davenports were not fools. They knew this action could bring a raiding party, but the entire community would be prepared for them. If the blue coats were foolish enough to ride in to Davenport country (as some folks put it), then it would be like a turkey shoot for the residents.

When Henry and Dan reached the house, John Carter was standing on the porch to greet them. John was surprised to see Henry. "You're as bad as your brother. Always showing up when yew ain't expected."

Henry embraced John, saying, "Yep, it's starting to be a habit. Folks will be starting a rumor about me fighting for the south or something." When some of the Davenports heard Henry say this, they laughed. They didn't have a clue that Henry was serious, but John knew.

"John, how is Eli?" Henry asked.

John lowered his head, saying, "We lost him just before all the shooting started. I'll be taking him home now and burying him next to his mother."

"I'm sorry John; I'm so sorry." Henry said.

One of the Davenport women walked out of the house and said, "There's vittles on the table, everyone."

"Thank you, ma'am," Henry said.

"Guess you'll be trying to find out about Thomas," John said.

"Yep. This sounds familiar. The first time I met you, I was looking for my brother," Henry said.

"This time, Henry, it looks like I won't be much help to you, but ol' Dan might give you a hand," John said.

Dan never said a word. He walked inside the house, sat down at the table, and began eating. "No, John," said Henry. "I'll go this thing alone. If I find him, I'll get him out somehow. But if I don't, I'll just go back home and pick up where I left off," Henry said, matter of factly. Both men stood silently, looking out across the pastures at the mountains.

"What are they gonna do with those men in the barn?" Henry asked.

"That's old man Davenport's worries, not mine, but he'll probably turn them over to Mosby's bunch. They'll know what to do with them."

"I've heard of him. Is he the one Thomas said pulled his bacon out of the fire when he got wounded?"

"The same," John responded.

"Dan told me about that fellow. Said he captured some high-ranking Yankee General not long ago. Boy, that must had been some ordeal," Henry whistled.

"They do a lot damage to fellows like that in the barn, so I've been told," John said.

"He and Thomas have something in common then, wouldn't you say?" Henry asked.

John turned to knock ash out of his pipe, before going inside the house, saying, "Henry, there are many like Mosby, including people like the Davenports."

Henry followed, stopping in the living room, and walked over to a long pine box that held the body of Eli Carter. He removed his hat and remembering what John told him about Simmons promising to hang him, Henry said quietly, "Well, Simmons, looks like you lied again."

Dan Holland had finished eating by the time Henry sat down. Excusing himself, Dan said, "I'll relieve the man that's guarding those prisoners. Henry, when you finish, come on out to the barn. Maybe those fellows know where they've taken your brother."

When Dan reached the barn, he found the door wide open and no one around. Near one of the stalls lay the motionless body of the guard. The prisoners had escaped out the back and into the thick forest. Dan tried to help the guard, but it was useless. He was dead.

Dan hurried back to the house shouting, "Saddle up boys! The Yanks have escaped!"

Everyone at the table scampered out the door and headed to their mounts. Old man Davenport shouted, "Hold it, fellows. Let's have some real fun. One of you go fetch those hounds and let them tell us where they are."

Hoping to pick up the prisoners scent, the old man led the dogs to where the prisoners had been.

"Couple of you fellows take old Charlie up to the house and put him on a cooling board. Then one of you go fetch his folks. They'll want to give him a proper burial.

The rest of you go with me; we'll catch those murdering bastards, if it's the last thing I do," growled the old man.

Henry stood silently, just watching the men mount. One of the Davenports asked, "You comin' with us Watkins, or you headin' out to find your brother?"

Looking directly at Henry, John Carter said, "I'm hoping he will help me take my boy home."

Henry knew John was full of surprises, so his response was, "Yep. I think I'll help John."

Greater Love Hath No Man

Chapter eleven

The journey to Carter Town would be long and slow-moving for John in the borrowed wagon. Henry agreed to ride along beside him until he reached his turn-off, and then he would attempt his homeward travel once again. Henry had learned to like John's dry humor and fatherly advice.

As they traveled, Henry asked, "When you were out west before the war, what did you do with those Indians?"

"What yew mean, do with 'em?" John replied.

"You know, fight Indians and all," Henry said.

John remained silent for several minutes before answering. "I lived with them for a spell, come to know their ways, even married one, but she didn't live long."

Henry waited before asking, "You ever have any kids by her?"

"No. Like I said, she didn't live very long after we married."

Henry could see John getting a little nervous. Both men sat quietly for several miles. Finally Henry said, "Pull up a minute John. I think my mare's reins are coming loose back there." John did as Henry asked. Henry turned around and reached over the casket, re-tying his horse's reins to the tailgate.

When they started traveling again, John changed the subject, saying, "That's a fine looking animal back there, Henry. You raise her from a colt?"

"Yep. She was so big at birth, I had to pull her. I lost her mama, though. A few times I thought I would lose her, but she managed to hang in there."

"You teach her the gaits?" John asked.

"Yep. That's what I like doing best," Henry answered.

The two men chatted all the way to the trail that led to Carter Town. "Well John, this is where I leave you. I'm sure sorry about Eli. You sure you'll make it home all right?" Henry asked.

"I'll be fine. You go on home to your family now, and if I hear anything about the Major, I'll let you know. Watch out for those boys dressed in blue. You might not be so lucky next time," John warned.

Mounting his gray, Henry waved as John drove the wagon on to the trail and out of sight.

Clouds were banking in the western sky, telling Henry it would be a dark and rainy night. If he were to continue riding the pike, he would be camping somewhere along the timberline. After riding about a mile, he felt raindrops falling on his hands. This was a sure sign he would be in for a wet night. In an hour the pike would be soggy mud and much too dangerous to travel. Finding a place where he could get out of the storm and light a fire was priority for now.

Riding to a knoll that had a several large oaks, he found an ideal camp site. At the base of the trees, large root knees were big enough to shield him and his horse from blowing winds. He quickly dismounted and tied his horse. He tossed his saddle near the base, between two root knees. Henry managed to find some dry leaves and twigs to start a fire.

As the fire started, he heard a wagon coming from the same direction he had just traveled. Thinking it might be John, he eased out to the edge of the pike. He discovered that it wasn't a wagon he heard but a cannon being pulled by two mules. There were several Confederate soldiers on horseback following.

They're sure in a powerful hurry, wherever they're going, Henry thought. Easing back to his camp site, he wrapped up in his blanket next to the fire. The rain was beginning to fall hard. The big oak he sat under acted as a leaky umbrella.

At times he thought he would lose his fire, but by throwing more dried wood on, it would soon catch up and burn much brighter.

Those fellows are getting their butts wet by now, Henry thought. He watched the rain fall against the ground until he drifted off to sleep. He was dreaming about home and his family and how they were fishing in Miller's Creek. When Mildred caught one so big it was pulling her in the creek, he woke up. Realizing it was only a dream, he sat smiling for a few minutes and soon drifted back to sleep.

In the wee hours, his horse snorted, waking him again. Peeking out the corner of one eye, he noticed the fire had died down to embers. He chugged it a couple of times, threw more wood on the embers and laid back down.

Henry was almost asleep when he heard a voice shouting, "Hello, in the camp!"

Reaching for his revolver, he stared into the darkness. He could hear brush moving, but the rain muffled the direction it was coming from. He waited patiently for the person to step out of the darkness before he moved a muscle. Henry could hear the person coming closer. Then, instantly the sound stopped. The tree roots shielded Henry, making it almost impossible to be seen from any direction. The rain had slowed to a drizzle.

"Okay to come to the fire?" came the voice again.

With the hammer cocked, Henry pointed his revolver toward the voice and said, "Okay, come on in!"

When the person stepped into the light, Henry could see it was just a boy, dressed in a ragged uniform of the Confederate army. A long knife hanging from his side seemed to be the only weapon he had.

"Toss that knife on the ground, and have a seat by the fire," Henry ordered. The lad did as he was told. Easing the hammer back in to a non-firing position, Henry placed his revolver back in its holster. Henry walked to the fire and looked at the boy. "Sure is a bad night for a boy to be wandering around in the forest. Especially without a gun, wouldn't you think?"

"I had one up 'till yesterday, but I run out of bullets; the blasted thing was too heavy to tote around empty, and beside I ain't no boy," the lad replied.

Henry determined him to be a southern deserter. "Don't suppose you have any vittles you'd want to share, do you?" The lad asked. Henry hated to tell him he had none.

"Where you from, partner?" Henry asked.

"Arkansas," the boy answered. "You a bounty hunter?"

Henry almost burst out laughing. "How old are you?" Henry asked.

"Eighteen," the lad responded.

"Naw. Yew ain't more'n fifteen," Henry grinned.

The warmth of the fire felt good to the boy's wet body, causing him to drift off to sleep.

Now what? Henry thought. It'll be daylight soon and if I'm caught again, especially with this kid, they'll hang me for certain. Henry let him sleep until dawn. Nudging the boys foot, he said, "I'll be leaving you now."

Raising his head, the lad asked, "Where ya headed?"

"Due west to a farm where a woman and two little girls await me," Henry answered. Henry mounted his gray and looked down at the boy. "You a farm boy?" he asked.

"Yes sir. Paw and my older brother and me raised cotton and sugar cane before joining up with General Lee's army."

"Where's your brother?" Henry asked.

"He got killed at Chancellorsville a few days ago, so I was heading home to help my Paw."

"Pick up your knife and give me your hand. This mare will double no farther than we're going," Henry ordered. The big gray carried the two down the road in a single foot pace.

"You never answered my question, mister," the boy said.

"What question was that?" Henry asked.

"Bounty hunter. Well, are you?"

Snickering, Henry responded, "Far from it, partner. Yep, far from it."

Loosening one arm from Henry's grip, the boy reached out his hand and introduced himself, "I'm Donald Henderson. Fellows in my company called me Little Arkie."

Greater Love Hath No Man

Shaking his hand, Henry said "Henry Watkins. Glad to know you, Little Arkie." They rode silently for several miles. "lets give the horse a rest, what ya say," Henry said.

"Sounds good to me. My butt feels like a busted stump," the lad answered.

Finding a good place to rest, Henry tied his mount to a nearby tree. "Ever raise any corn back where you come from?" asked Henry.

"Raised some for the table and some for the hogs, but mostly cotton," the boy answered.

"I thought slaves did all the work in the cotton fields, and the land owner just managed the crop. Or that's what some folks did around here."

"We've never owned no slaves, but old man Hunter did," the boy said.

"Who's old man Hunter?" Henry asked.

"He was a neighbor of ours. Paw didn't like him much. Said he was mean to his darkies and that somebody ought to take him out and horse whup him, just like he done to those slaves of his, and you know one hot night, they did just that. Three men with black hoods over their heads took him out, stretched him over a wagon wheel and tore the hide right off'n his back. Paw said he was down for several weeks mending. Folks just didn't accept all that kind of stuff too well back home," the boy explained.

"If your family felt that way about slavery, then why in thunder would you and your brother join an army to fight for slavery?" Henry questioned.

"Oh, we didn't join to fight for no slave stuff. We joined, because they said that folks up north was coming to take our lands."

Henry shook his head saying, "Well, if that don't beat all." Henry was starting to like this boy. "Now, do you want to tell me the truth about your age?" Henry asked.

"Fifteen, but I'll be sixteen in December," the boy answered.

Henry thought to himself, *I bet this boy's parents are worried sick over him.*

When the rest period was over, the two traveled on toward the Watkins farm.

Barking dogs warned Mildred of Henry's arrival. She called to the girls, "Your father is home!"

With arms wide open, the girls ran out the back door shouting, "Daddy! Daddy!"

Henry leaped off the big gray, leaving the young lad still seated. Bending down and pulling both girls to his bosom, Henry hugged them tightly, kissing them on their foreheads.

Gladys looked up at the boy and asked, "Who's that, daddy?"

"Well it's a long story, bright eyes. I'll let you meet him over supper."

Holding her nose, while looking at Violet, Gladys said, "Mama is standing on the porch waiting, Daddy."

"We better go draw some water and fill up the tub before Mama tells us to," said Henry grinning from ear to ear.

Mildred stood patiently waiting, with both hands on her hips. With a big smile, Henry reached to pick her up, as always, but not before she handed him a bar of lye soap.

"Pew! You're ripe!" she said.

"Yep. The girls just let me know."

"Who you got with you?" Mildred asked. Henry motioned for the lad to come and meet his family.

"Why, he's just a boy!" Mildred said.

"Begging the lady's pardon, ma'am, but I'm a solider," the lad said proudly.

Smiling while looking at Henry, she asked, "Okay. Is that a southern uniform you're wearing?"

"Yes, ma'am, and proud of it," the boy growled.

Winking at Henry, she responded sharply, "Well, Johnnie Reb, I bet you're hungry."

"Mrs. Watkins, I would like for you to meet my young friend, Arkie Henderson. He hails from the big state of Arkansas. Arkie, this is Mrs. Watkins, my wife, and this little bright-eyed girl here is my daughter Gladys, and my other daughter, Violet. Family, meet Arkie Henderson, from Arkansas. He will be a guest for a day or two."

Violet handed him a bar of soap and said, "After Daddy, you can go." Not waiting to be told, the girls scampered out the back door to stable the big gray.

Chapter twelve

Warm baths and late visitation caused the male occupants of the Watkins house to sleep as soundly as babies, while several miles away, near Fairfax, a Confederate Major sat in a tree, waiting for daylight. Thomas Watkins had managed to escape from his imprisonment. He knew it would be dangerous traveling the pike. The guards had stripped him of everything, except his shirt and trousers, leaving him barefooted as well.

When dawn came, he managed to get to the edge of the pike and walk the timberline west, toward Carter Town. With his feet bleeding, it would be a slow pace. In his warfare experience, he had made many enemies, but his friends outnumbered them by far.

He reached an opening where he could walk the pike and see for several yards either way, in case he had to dart back into the timberline and hide. The road was hard and dusty but much easier on his feet. It seemed like he had been walking for hours when he heard the rumble of a wagon coming from behind him. Thomas dashed into the timbers and hid where he could see the wagon, which was loaded down with all sorts of goods. He knew that wherever a sutler wagon was, Federals were close by.

When the wagon passed, his thought was to run to the back and bluff his way through a robbery. As he was coming out of the woods, a column of Federal troops approached, forcing the wagon to the side of the road. It was a long column, and they were pulling several cannons and spoiling for a fight.

Thomas tried to see what division they were from. He lay motionless as several cavalrymen rode within a few feet of him. He watched as their flag bearers passed, telling him all he wanted to know.

He held his head down and tried breathing through his shirt sleeve because of the dust. When they passed, leaving their cloud of dust, Thomas looked as though he had bathed in talcum powder. The wagon remained stationary for several minutes, waiting for the dust to settle.

Thomas eased to the rear of the wagon and crouched behind the driver and in a whisper, said "Don't move a muscle or I'll blow you off that wagon seat!"

The driver never twitched. "Now, take out that sidearm and hold it by the barrel. Hand it back to me real slow. If you turn around, you'll meet your Maker."

The driver did as he was told, and Thomas took the revolver and pointed it at the driver. Then Thomas climbed onto the wagon. "Now, turn this wagon around and drive due west up the pike." The driver did as he was ordered, without a word. "You got any boots on this thing that'll fit me?" The driver didn't answer, so Thomas looked through several pairs, looking for something in his size.

The driver glanced at Thomas as he tried on boots. "Yore damned feet are swol' up, you ort to try putting some socks on," grumbled the driver.

"Where's the New York cavalry headed?" Thomas asked.

"Don't know. Why didn't you stop 'em and ask?" The driver growled.

Thomas found socks and boots that fit.

"You know, you could save yourself some trouble if you tell me where the New York is headed." The driver never said a word. Thomas, getting angry with the man, ordered him to pull the wagon to a stop.

Cocking the pistol and putting it to the driver's head, Thomas said, "Leaving your ass here for the buzzards won't bother me one bit fellow, so I'll ask you one more time. Where is the New York headed?"

"Johnnie Reb, I don't know for sure. They been chasing you for a long time now, and they almost made it work at the crossroads, but you fellers are slicker 'n axle grease."

"Get this thing going, and when you reach the road that leads to Carter Town, take it," Thomas ordered.

"You might as well shoot me now, and get it over with than make me go there!" the driver said.

"You know, partner, you might live to tell your grandchildren about all this, if you cooperate, " Thomas argued.

"I got a confession to make to you, Johnny. When you come up on me back there, you scared the hell out of me so bad, I swallered my chew, and I been sicker than hell the whole time, or I might been a little more friendlier," whined the driver. Thomas just grinned.

When they reached the Carter Town cut-off, Thomas ordered the driver off the wagon. "Will you give me a chance to pray before you shoot me?" the driver cried.

"Stop this wagon, and walk over to that tree, and start your prayers," Thomas ordered.

While the man knelt down and began praying, Thomas drove away. Looking back, Thomas shouted, "Looks like the good Lord heard your prayer, partner!"

At the home of Dr. Glass, Bonner was hitching the buggy when he saw the wagon pull up at the front of the house. He stopped what he was doing and walked to the house, thinking he would scold the driver and order him off the premises. When Thomas jumped down from the wagon, Bonner asked, "Major Thomas, sir. Is dat you?"

"None other, Bonner," grinned Thomas. "Is Miss Caroline at home?"

"Yes, sir. I was just fixing to hitch up the buggy for her. Major, what is you doing in those old rags?" Bonner asked.

"Smelly, too; it's a long story" Thomas replied.

"Come with me, Major, and I will draw your bath water. There's some more of them kind of uniforms you left in the guest room. Let me fetch them after your bath, and I will tell Miss Caroline you are home. I know you don't want her to see you like this," Thomas followed Bonner to the house.

When Bonner told Caroline of the arrival of Thomas and that he was in the bath, she ran to the guestroom. Not caring that Thomas was naked in the tub, she threw her arms around him and began kissing the side of his head as tears flowed freely from her eyes.

Bonner watched the two embrace. He smiled as he closed the door and began humming a happy tune as he walked down the hallway.

That evening at supper, Thomas looked very handsome. He was dressed in a Confederate officer's uniform. He shined as if he were attending a ball at the capitol in Richmond. Word had spread throughout the town of his arrival. Several of his peers had joined them at the table; Dr. Glass sat at the head as the host. John Carter was the first to rise and toast the safe return of Thomas. Others joined in the toast immediately.

Before the main course was served, the room became silent as Thomas began the story of his escape.

Looking at Caroline, he began, "As some of you may know, I left here to support General Lee's command at Chancellorsville by giving strength to those on the Orange. We were engaged as soon as we reached the area. It was there that my good friend John Carter lost his son Eli, while performing what I call an outstanding heroic deed for his country."

Tearfully, Thomas told how all the men performed gallantly. John Carter never took his eyes off Thomas as Thomas continued to explain what he understood of the battle:

"It appeared that the Yankees were trying to send reinforcements to Hooker at Chancellorsville, when Wilcox and his boys of General Early's division changed their plans. I'm here to tell you, we put those fellows dressed in blue to praying over near Salem church.

"Along about nightfall General Lee sent some help. Wilcox and his men sent those Yankees packing across two pontoon bridges at Scott's Dam. We poured the grape shot to them. I'm not sure, but I think this had a bearing on Hooker and his bunch hightailing back across the Rappahannock.

"Later the next day, thinking I could get a firsthand glimpse of the retreat, I followed a back trail. I sent my men back with the report, and I stayed to watch with my field glass. A handful of straggling yanks eased up behind me. These boys were so scared, that at the least bit of resistance they would have shot me.

"After they stripped me of everything but my shirt and trousers, they all went to sleep, including the guard. I managed to untie my hands by using my teeth and I hightailed it out of there. Crawling off into the woods and shinnying up a tree was probably the best thing I could have done. When those yanks woke up, they never looked in my direction.

"What I regret most of all is that I should have recovered my property before I left. But I guess if I would have done that, I wouldn't be here today, giving you this report."

When Thomas finished talking, everyone in the room held their glasses high and cheered, "Hip, hip, and hooray!"

When the dinner was over, everyone gathered in the parlor where some of the local citizens had prepared music for their entertainment. Thomas and Caroline excused themselves and walked to the terrace. A touch of fragrance from an apple orchard in bloom seemed to embrace the couple in a way they wished would never end.

Thomas looked at Caroline and kissed her gently. Her elegance and beauty could not be described. She was dressed in a floor-length blue silk gown, supported by hoops and stays, and her eyes sparkled. Her long shiny hair was decorated with brightly colored hairpins. It was an evening they would always remember.

As the two embraced, Thomas asked, "Should we tell them of our engagement tonight?"

"Why don't we wait until this war is over before we announce our intention," she replied.

Thomas walked to the railing and stared out into the night. "Is there something troubling you?" he asked.

Caroline paused before answering, "I have been corresponding with Rose, while she has been imprisoned, and she tells me that there is talk about releasing her to the southern states. If that happens, she plans a trip to Europe."

"What's that got to do with us?" Thomas asked.

"Before you came, Bonner was preparing for my departure to Richmond. President Davis has requested my presence as soon as possible."

They could hear the music as it began playing an old familiar waltz. Thomas smiled and said, "May I have this dance?" It seemed they danced for hours. When the music stopped Thomas said, "You'll need an escort."

"No, that won't be necessary, and besides Bonner and I have traveled this road several times in the past two years; I'll be just fine," she answered. "Our guests await us, Major. Shall we go inside and be sociable?" She smiled.

When they entered the room, John Carter approached and said to Thomas, "There are several men awaiting orders. What should I tell them?"

"I'll meet with them later. Right now, let's enjoy our party," Thomas answered.

Approaching Caroline, Dr. Glass asked, "Do you suppose an old man might rate a dance with the most beautiful girl in the world?"

Smiling while glancing at Thomas, she remarked, "I'm sure the Major won't mind, being that it's you."

Looking toward the punch bowl, John Carter said, "What say we get something to drink?"

An hour later the grandfather clock chimed the morning in, and the party broke up, leaving Thomas and Caroline alone on the settee.

The party had been just what the community needed after suffering Simmons' ordeal. In the wee hours, Thomas snoozed with his head in Caroline's lap.

He never woke up as Bonner walked quietly into the room and nudged Caroline's foot. "We is all set. You need to change clothes while I bring the buggy around front," he whispered.

Caroline gently moved Thomas' head on to the cushion without disturbing him. She and Bonner had been gone two hours before Thomas knew she had left.

The sound of glasses rattling brought Thomas to his feet. Bonner's family was cleaning the room where he slept.

When Thomas realized that Caroline had gone, he dashed out of the room and summoned for one of Bonner's children to bring John Carter. While he waited for John, he walked to the terrace. Remembering the night and what Caroline had told him just hours before kindled an anger inside that made him clutch his fist and hit the palm of his other hand.

John came to Thomas and watched him pace back and forth. "You wanted to see me, Major?" he asked.

"If those men are ready, I'll meet with them now," Thomas replied.

"They are at the stable, " John answered

The local stable was under construction, because it had become damaged from the Simmons raid. Forrest Atkins was the smithy. He was a big burly fellow who always wore sleeveless shirts and was always in need of a bath.

As the men gathered, he let it be known that if they were going after Simmons, he was going with them. Knowing that Atkins held a personal grudge, Thomas would never let him do that. He was much more valuable to the citizens of Carter Town.

Twelve men sat waiting as John Carter and Thomas walked through the doorway. "Gentlemen, I hope I haven't kept you waiting too long," Thomas said.

John began introducing some of the new faces among the group, while those who had ridden with Thomas before greeted him with happiness.

Thomas began by explaining what John had told him about the Davenport fight. "Gentlemen, you might ought to know that the Yankees won't take this lightly. As I told some of you last night, how we sent those boys packing back across the river. I'm here to tell you, they will be back, so we have a choice.

"General Lee gave them fellows a good whooping at Chancellorsville, and old Abe won't stand for that, either. So between going up and helping the Davenports or staying here waiting for Simmons, knowing he may never come, what do you think we should do?"

One of the men asked, "Sir, does anyone know you're here, yet?"

"When a certain person reaches Richmond, I'm sure we will receive orders as to what to do," Thomas answered.

Everyone knew whom he was talking about. "Then we will wait and do what our hands find to do, is that right?" John Carter asked.

Thomas was delighted to see John take an active part. Thomas ended the meeting: "Then it's settled; everyone will go back to doing what each man was doing, and when I get word I'll let you know."

Greater Love Hath No Man

Chapter thirteen

Several miles into their trip, Bonner pulled the team to a complete stop. "Miss Caroline," said Bonner, "we need to rest the horses for now. We will be at the Red Rooster Inn soon, and once there, you'll have a bed to rest in and a hot bath."

Caroline was half asleep as she looked out and tried to determine where they were. "This is Elms Crossing. We've stopped here before, haven't we?" she asked.

As Bonner unhitched the horses from the buggy and tied them to a nearby tree, he answered, "Yes ma'am. It's only about an hour from here to the inn."

Caroline needed to stretch her legs. She got out and walked awhile, remembering the last time they had stopped here. Pointing toward a slope, she asked, "Wasn't there a spring that fed a little waterfall over their somewhere?"

Bonner looked where she pointed. "Looks like a lot of underbrush done covered it up. I'll go see for you." He walked through the underbrush and stopped quickly. He knew better than to let his mistress see what he had found.

"No, ma'am. Looks like the thing dried up. I believe these horses have had their rest for now. We might ought to get on to the inn if I'm gonna get you a room for the night," he said. He hurriedly hitched the team to the buggy and drove them quickly down the road.

"Bonner, what did you see back there?" she asked. Bonner pretended not to hear her. Caroline repeated, "I said, what did you see back there?"

"Now, Miss Caroline, you know your father wouldn't want you looking at some dead men; why he'd skin me alive if'n I allowed that," he answered.

Several minutes later, she asked, "Were they our boys or yanks?"

Bonner was much too smart to trap himself by taking sides. Acting scared, he answered, "Really couldn't tell. I didn't want to stay long enough to see."

"Yeah, I noticed," Caroline said and smiled.

Red Rooster Inn was known for being a good and clean place to rest. Since the Confederacy had moved their capitol to Richmond, the inn rarely had vacancies. When they arrived, a well-groomed black man assisted Bonner with Caroline's luggage.

When she walked inside, the assistant said to Bonner, "Nigger, what's wrong with you? Bringing Miss Caroline through Elms Crossing! Didn't you know they had a battle up there the other day, and the Johnny Rebels left a lot of dead Yanks lying around? We could see the buzzards circling from here."

"I saw some, but she didn't," Bonner answered.

Mr. Charles Barnes, the owner of the inn, greeted Caroline, and as always showed her to her room, personally. "The girls will have your bath ready for you soon. Will you be staying long?" He asked.

"Just for the night. We will be leaving at dawn," she answered.

"Your father, Dr. Glass, is he well?" Barnes asked.

With a pleasant smile, she answered, "Quite well. Thank you."

As Mr. Barnes was leaving he asked, "Will you be dining with us, or shall I have something brought to your room? And by the way, there's a gentleman who wishes to speak with you. What should I tell him?"

Pausing for a moment, she replied, "After I freshen up, I'll take my meal in the dining room. You may tell the gentleman he may speak to me there."

"Very well, Miss Caroline. I shall tell him." Barnes bowed politely and left the room to return to the front desk. In the entertainment room, a musical band was preparing the guests for a surprise.

When Caroline entered the dining room wearing a full length daffodil yellow satin dress, everyone in the room stared. She was definitely the center of attention. As she waited to be seated, a distinguished looking, well-dressed young man approached her, carrying a top hat.

"May I?" he asked, as he pulled the chair out for her to sit. Laying his hat in a vacant chair next to them he asked, "Might I have a word with you?"

Caroline smiled, giving him permission to be seated. "Allow me to introduce myself, Miss Glass. I'm Wilton Plummer from Richmond, and I have a message for you."

Caroline was surprised. "You have a message for me?" she asked.

"It's not a written message, however. President Davis has asked me to try and make contact with you before reaching Richmond, and being aware of your travels, I was in hope of reaching you here."

"Mr. Plummer, that is your name?" she asked. "How is it that you know so much about me and I know nothing of you?"

He assured Caroline that he was telling the truth by showing her documents that proved his identity, and she invited him to join her for dinner. During the meal, there were discussions of how badly the war was going for the south, and the need of gold for goods from Europe was the main topic.

After they finished dinner ,the sound of music coming from the entertainment room sent them to the doorway for a glimpse of "Camptown Races" being performed by white men wearing black face paint and singing like Negroes.

"Shall we go in and enjoy the minstrel show?" Mr. Plummer asked.

"By all means," she replied. They watched acts such as old folks at home and listened to riddles, puns, and comedic one liners. It was a delight to all.

When the show closed with some of Stephen Fosters' songs, people started returning to their rooms, whistling and singing the same tunes.

"Well, Mr. Plummer, I might say that was a treat. It's good to see that attitude once again in our midst, instead of the boring daily remarks about the ongoing war," Caroline said.

"Miss Caroline, the parlor is open. May we go inside and finish our business?" he asked.

Even though he had shown documents stating who he was, she still didn't trust him. "Let me get this right. I'm to abort the trip to Richmond and accompany you to

Washington to Rose's home in your coach. Is that right?" She asked.

"Yes. That's correct," he said, then smiled.

"What about Bonner and my property?" she responded. Caroline knew through corresponding with Rose that she was under house arrest and was imprisoned in her own home. "Rose. Is she well and still free to mingle in her circle of influence?" she asked.

Plummer's response made her decision for her. "Oh yes. She has remained above suspicion so far, and that's why you are needed. President Davis wants you to work with her there."

"Well Mr. Plummer, what time should we depart in the morning?" she asked.

"After we have eaten, if that's all right," he responded.

"It's late and time for my rest now, so until the morning at breakfast, I'll bid you a good night, Mr. Plummer," she said.

Caroline knew that Plummer was mistaken or lying about Rose and her confinement. She quickly changed clothes, left through the back door, and walked to the stables. Bonner saw her when she entered.

"Why, Miss Caroline! What's wrong? Why are you here?"

"Never mind," she scolded. "I'll hitch up the buggy, while you go fetch my luggage out of my room. And make sure no one sees you. Is that understood"?

Bonner did as he was told. When he returned with her luggage, Caroline was seated in the buggy, waiting. "Bonner, call that Negro over there and tell him to give this letter to Mr. Barnes in the morning. It has some money in it, and he better give it to him, or I'll come back here and horsewhip him," she said.

"Yes, ma'am. You won't have no problem out of old Moses. He'll do it," Bonner replied.

Greater Love Hath No Man

The night was clear and the pike was dry. "Miss Caroline, you care to tell old Bonner what's the matter?"

"Just drive the horses," she replied. When daylight came, it was still more than a day's journey to Richmond, and the horses were tired.

Caroline tried sleeping, but it seemed Bonner found every hole on the pike. "Pull off the pike and into that clump of trees so we all can get some rest," she ordered. As always, Bonner did as he was told.

He unhitched the team and haltered them so they could graze the damp grass. He spread a blanket down under a big elm for Caroline to lie on and placed one of her bags near the tree trunk for a pillow.

He said, "It ain't home, but it'll do until I can get you to Richmond."

When Caroline placed her head on the bag, she quickly dozed off to sleep. That left Bonner stretched out in the buggy.

The sun was at high noon when Caroline woke up. She walked over to the buggy and looked at Bonner, as he held his head down on the edge of the seat. She nudged his foot. "Bet you have a crick in your neck, sleeping like that," Caroline said and chuckled.

Bonner quickly jumped out of the buggy. "Miss Caroline, sho' is good to hear you back to your old self," Bonner said, then grinned.

"I was just tired. I didn't mean to be short with you," she responded.

"Oh, that's all right. Old Bonner knows when you've been troubled."

"You sure no one saw you get my things out of my room?" she asked.

"Yes ma'am. Quite sure," Bonner answered.

"How far would you say we are from Richmond now?"

"More than a day's ride, I'd say. Now Miss Caroline, what's ailing you child? You know you can tell old Bonner. I was there when the doctor spanked your bottom the first day you took a breath, girl."

"Yes, I've been told that a thousand times or more," she said. Caroline showed worry by biting her fingernails.

"Miss Caroline, don't you be biting them nasty fingernails. You knows what your father says about how it causes a person to be wormy!" scolded Bonner.

Caroline watched as Bonner hitched the team to the buggy. "More than a day's ride, you say?" she asked.

"Yes ma'am. Closer to two days," Bonner replied. He knew that whatever happened at the Red Rooster Inn had definitely caused a fear in her.

Softly she asked, "Bonner, when you and Mama Bonner got married, what was it like?"

"What you mean, child?"

"Was Mama Bonner excited?"

"Child, when your father bought Mama Bonner that day at the auction block, I couldn't keep my eyes off her, and you knows it has been like that for nearly forty years now." He smiled, as he remembered.

"My mother. What was she like?" asked Caroline.

"Like you, child. Jus' like you," he responded.

"Was she pretty? Were she and my father happy?" she asked.

"Happy? Why child, when yo' Mama found out she was going to have you, Lawd, she was the happiest person in the whole wide world."

"How did she die? Was it because she had me? Father refuses to tell me."

"No, child. Yo' poppa blames himself for not knowing more about doctoring than he does. It was a sickness that nobody knew what to do about. It was called scarlet fever. Your father wrote different schools for answers, but nothing came," Bonner replied.

Greater Love Hath No Man

"Turn this buggy around Bonner! We're going home!" she cried.

Chapter fourteen

There was a great deal of excitement at the Red Rooster Inn as Bonner stopped the buggy and helped Caroline out. The same well-groomed Negro that assisted the day before offered his help once again. "What's all the commotion about?" Bonner asked.

"I tell you later," he whispered, as he carried Caroline's luggage inside.

Charles Barnes saw her as she entered the room. "Why, Miss Caroline, you left in such a hurry I didn't get a chance to speak to you again," he said.

"You did get your money, didn't you?" she asked.

Greater Love Hath No Man

"Why, yes. Moses brought it to me along with your note of apology," he answered.

"What has happened? Why are all these so people troubled?" she asked.

"We have had a shooting not more than an hour ago. Tragedy, just plain tragedy! That's what it is!" Barnes cried.

"Who was shot? And what was it all about?" she asked.

"Do you remember that fine looking gentleman that dined with you last night? A Mr. Plummer? Well, about an hour ago, a tall man I have never seen before, dressed in a very stylish suit, just walked up and shot him while he sat looking out the window. Apparently for no reason. Just plain murder! That's what it is, just plain murder!"

Quickly changing the subject, Barnes asked, "You will be staying with us tonight in spite of what's happened, won't you?"

"Why, of course," answered Caroline. "Has anyone claimed his body, yet?"

"Yes. Two men claiming to be related came and carried it away in a wagon not more than five minutes before you and your Negro drove up," Barnes answered.

Realizing that Plummer had lied about Rose made Caroline more comfortable about leaving in the middle of the night and she felt fortunate to still be alive. Her correspondence with Wild Rose and the information she received about large Federal troop movements had brought victories to the south many times.

It was common knowledge that General Beauregard of the Southern Command gave Rose's network credit for winning the battle of Manassas.

But Caroline wanted out. The month of June was here, and she wished to be a bride. As she lay in bed that night, her thoughts ran wildly on how the Federals had planned to trap her or perhaps even kill her. *Did President*

Davis really send for me or was that bait? she wondered. Gratefully, she prayed as she drifted off to sleep.

The following morning, things were as quiet as a graveyard when she sat down for breakfast. Everyone in the room stared at her as though she may have something to do with Plummer's death. She ignored them and ordered her meal.

Charles Barnes had heard some of their whispering and went to her table and asked if he might join her. "By all means," she responded.

"Miss Caroline, I hope you won't think I'm in opposition of you being here, but some of the people seem to think you may... Oh, you know what I mean!" He exclaimed.

"Don't trouble yourself, Mr. Barnes. Bonner and I will be leaving as soon as I gather my things and pay my bill," she said sternly.

She finished her meal and walked to the front desk. She glanced at the door and noticed Bonner motioning for her to come. "What's wrong?" She asked.

"I have already gathered up your belongings, and they is in the buggy waiting on you," he said.

As she tried to pay her bill, the clerk said, "Your bill has been paid, Miss Caroline."

"By whom?" She asked.

"Some fellow wearing one of those new style hats paid it for you. Said he was an old friend," explained the desk clerk. Caroline walked outside to the buggy.

"Miss Caroline, you knows going on these here trips have always been exciting, but I believe this trip has the smell of the sweet potato," said Bonner.

"You're right, Bonner. It has been kind of a smelly thing at that," Caroline said and chuckled.

As they traveled on the return trip, Caroline noticed they were on a back trail, which ran near Cedar Creek. "Why did you take this route, Bonner? We could make better time going back the same way we came, through Elms Crossing," she said.

Bonner did not respond.

Caroline cleared her throat saying, "Bonner! I said, 'why did we take this route?'"

Bonner finally answered, "Miss Caroline, have you ever knowed old Bonner to let you down?"

"No, of course not, but what has that got to do with the way we are traveling?" she asked. As they approached a bend in the road, Bonner pointed to a clump of trees, "That's why," he said.

There, seated in a buggy, was a nicely dressed man, wearing a new style hat, just as the desk clerk had described.

Reaching in her handbag and pulling out a small Derringer, Caroline prepared herself for the worst. "You won't need that. It's not what you think," Bonner exclaimed.

The gentleman got out of his buggy and walked to where Caroline and Bonner had stopped. "Miss Glass, I hope you will forgive all of this secrecy for now, but its imperative that I speak with you," he said. "allow me to introduce myself. I'm Thaddeus Wilcox. I have come from Richmond to speak with you."

"No thanks, Mr. Wilcox, or whatever you call yourself. The last time I was approached by a stranger, he was dead in less than twenty fours hours."

"I'm afraid that was my doing. You see, the Federals have known of your operation for quite some time now and they have been under the impression that you may have passed on information that caused their defeats at Fredericksburg and Chancellorsville" he stated.

"So, they wanted me out of the way! Is that right?" she asked.

"Precisely," he responded.

Bonner interrupted, "You can trust this one, child. Moses knows who he is, and he told me to come this way so you two can meet."

Caroline took a deep breath and put the Derringer back in her handbag. "Then, Mr. Wilcox, if Bonner has endorsed our meeting, I'm willing to listen," she said.

"Well, first of all we are aware of your involvement with Major Thomas Watkins, and let me offer my personal congratulations on your upcoming marriage. Now, we have reason to believe that there is a huge Federal movement on the way to Culpepper County, and we have several infantry corps in that region, even General Lee himself. We would like to know the whereabouts of that large movement and who is leading it."

Caroline stared at the ground and thought before saying, "How many days do I have to get you this information?"

"Three, at the most," he replied.

"How will I get you this information?" she asked.

Wilcox pointed toward the creek bed as several men dressed in Confederate cavalry uniforms came riding up. "That big Major wearing those plume feathers in his hat, leading these men, will most likely be the one to receive your message," he said and smiled.

When she saw Thomas, Caroline leaped out of the buggy and ran to him with tears streaming down her cheeks.

Bonner watched as she hurried to greet him. Wiping tears from his own eyes, he said, "Da Lawd sho' moves in mysterious ways, don't he, Mr. Wilcox?"

"Yes, he does, Bonner. Indeed he does," he replied.

Greater Love Hath No Man

Chapter fifteen

The railhead was fifteen miles away, and Caroline needed to send a coded telegram to Washington. They met with no opposition.

Since the mosquitoes were horrible, Thomas bivouacked his troops in a small valley away from the creek. They would wait there for her return. Thomas was aware of the dangers of her mission. If she were caught, it would probably mean prison or perhaps her life.

When she reached the depot, her message was sent. It read:

Greater Love Hath No Man

"My dearest uncle, although you have allowed yourself to become a shut-in, mother has still requested your presence at once. There will be several coming to the gathering but not sure how many. She wishes for you to be there, anyway. Waiting for your immediate reply. Signed, your loving family member."

The telegrapher sent the message, and while they were waiting for an answer, Federal troops rode by. Smiling, the officer in charge tipped his hat at Caroline as they passed. In about an hour, a response came. She folded the telegram and placed it in her drawstring handbag. She then walked to the buggy. Bonner never said a word as he drove the team back to the main road. He ran the horses at a full pace for several miles before stopping to rest.

After the battle of Fredericksburg, many deserters from both sides traveled the pike. Scallywags would lie in wait, hoping to find some poor soul they could steal from.

While the horses were resting, Bonner dozed off to sleep, only to be aroused by the sound of brush moving close by. Glancing out the corner of one eye, he could see Caroline with her eyes shut.

"I hear it," she whispered.

Bonner always kept a loaded ten-gauge shotgun on the floor, under his feet. The sound was coming closer. Bonner picked up the gun and laid it in his lap. Both barrels were cocked.

Caroline reached into her handbag and cocked the hammer back on a double-shot Derringer. They were ready.

Bonner could hear whispers but couldn't quite hear what they were saying. Both Caroline and Bonner pretended to be a sleep.

"I can shoot that nigger from here," whispered a voice from the brush.

"I ain't never shot no woman before. You shoot the woman, and I'll shoot the nigger," another voice whispered.

"Why we need to shoot that pretty woman for? Let's shoot the nigger and see what's under all them petticoats first."

Easing up behind the buggy, the two Yankee deserters crouched, hoping to get an advantage. As they reached the rear of the buggy, Bonner whirled and pulled the trigger on one barrel, sending a load of buck shot into the face of one of the assailants. His partner saw what was happening and started running through the forest. Bonner sent a load of buckshot in his direction.

"You all right, Miss Caroline?" he asked.

Easing the hammer down on the derringer, she said, "I'm fine. How about yourself?"

"Seems like those blue boys knows a lot about running. I sent the other one through the woods with a load of buckshot in his hind quarters," Bonner said and laughed.

"Fredericksburg gave them a lot of practice, I hear," Caroline commented.

"Yes, ma'am, but that one over there gonna get to try out his legs with the devil and those buzzards up there, circling," Bonner answered.

He reloaded the shotgun and returned it to a spot under the seat. "If we gonna make it to the Major with your message, we best be going, wouldn't you think?" Bonner asked.

"Wake me when we get there," she said.

"Aw, Miss Caroline, you ain't gonna leave old Bonner to sing to himself all the way there, are you?"

"You'll do fine, Bonner. Besides, I like your singing. Especially that one you always sang at home about camptown races," she said.

As he drove the buggy onto the pike, Bonner smiled and said, "Aw, Miss Caroline, if you ain't something."

Greater Love Hath No Man

He could be heard for a half-mile or more, over and over. "Camp town racetrack, five miles long, doo dah, doo dah."

When he would get to the five miles long part he'd say, "And dees hosses can't run no five-mile track without stopping."

Caroline would burst out laughing. This went on for several miles, until Caroline finally said, "Sing a different one. You've worn me out on that one."

"I got one you gonna like. It's the new one everybody's singing. Oh, I wish I was in Dixie, hooray, hooray."

Caroline sat up and said, "Bonner, you are in Dixie, and you ain't never picked a pound of cotton in your whole life."

"Yes, ma'am, you're right, but old Moses has. He told me about the place down in Mississippi where he and his family was born. Said they were mean to them. He said dey whup his poppa till there's nothing but scars on his back."

"People like that get what's coming to them, sooner or later," Caroline answered.

"Yes, ma'am. I hear tell the Butchers over at Butcher's tavern done got theirs, some says," he answered.

"Well, you're free, and all your family is free born, so sing something else," she said.

Bonner continued humming the doo dah tune as the horses carried them down the road. About a mile from the trail that led to the campsite, two of Thomas' men came up and rode along side the buggy. "Is everything all right?" asked Caroline.

"Yes ma'am," he replied. "I think the Major has a surprise for you." The two horsemen rode up front, leading the way. When they entered the camp, Thomas was standing in front of his tent. Bonner stopped the buggy directly in front of him.

Caroline got out, while Bonner drove the buggy away, leaving the two embracing each other. Caroline handed Thomas the telegram.

"Let's go inside," he said. Reading the telegram and trying to understand, he said, "You'll have to interpret this. It don't make sense," he grumbled.

"Uncle sends this message as a general reply. He says he is enjoying pleasant weather there and was told only eight or ten families would be at the gathering. However, he would try to make it by the tenth and that he would come up the Rappahannock, so someone should be there to greet him." Caroline smiled and said, "General Pleasanton is in route with 8,000 to 10,000 men and should be somewhere near the Rappahannock River around the tenth of the month."

Thomas sat at the small table and pounded his fist against the top. "Well, by grabs, there will be someone there to greet him. From the last report I have, General Stuart is near Brandy Station, so that means Lee isn't far away. Wherever Lee is, Ewell and Longstreet will be there.

"That leaves Rooney Lee. Heaven only knows where he is. Yep, old uncle is going to be greeted in a big way, and there is little we can do to help." He knew it would be a good fight and an excellent opportunity for some of his younger troops to get some experience. Little did he know that he was going to miss the greatest cavalry battle of the war.

Caroline read the expression of disappointment in his eyes. As he pulled her close, he said, "You done real good, sweetheart, but with today being the eighth, there's no way we could get to Culpepper County in time. Our horses would be useless by then."

From outside the tent, Thomas' first sergeant called out, "Sir, the water is ready for the lady's bath."

"Good!" Thomas answered. "bring everything in."

Greater Love Hath No Man

Two men carried a round wooden tub into the tent, and two others brought buckets of hot water, filling the tub half full.

"Where did you find a tub out here?" asked Caroline, as the men prepared the bath.

"Compliments of the Red Rooster Inn, madam," mocked Thomas, bowing low.

"Hmmm... Moses, no doubt," she said.

"No doubt at all," he responded.

"Well, you be sure to thank him for me the very next time you see him," purred Caroline.

While she soaked in the hot water, Thomas joined his men. "First sergeant!" he bellowed, "are all the sentries posted and secure?"

"Yes, sir!" answered the sergeant. "I have posted the men personally."

Thomas nodded his assent and looked across the camp at his troopers. There were some that were too young for the army and several older veterans who had seen as much combat as Thomas had.

He was very proud of his men. They fought fiercely and bravely for a ragtag group. He strolled through the camp. With his tunic unbuttoned and his famous hat in his tent, one would have to look closely to recognize him. There were small fires with groups sitting around talking of home and of the war. He approached one group who seemed to be really having a good time. Quietly, Thomas sat on a log behind them, listening to the conversation.

"Yeah! Well just listen to this," said a young farm boy. "I was soft on Betty Jo Brubaker back home, and I wanted to make a good impression on her. I went to see her one Sunday afternoon, and as I walked up, her big old sow tore down a fence and run off into the woods.

"I commenced to run after her, and after a while I seen her just standing by a tree. I snuck up behind her and made a diving grab for her hind leg. I got a good grip, and that old sow took off like a shot, shakin' her hind leg like a cat that done stepped in pine tar.

"I swear, she musta' dragged me a quarter mile, still shaking that leg. Then she jumped a root, and I didn't. I woke up 'bout a hour later and wandered back to apologize for not catching the hog. That old sow was back in the pen, lying in the mud, pretty as you please. I never did go back to see Betty Jo after that."

When the laughter died down, an older trooper spoke up.

"Fellers, when I was just a whelp, my granddaddy took me to a brush arbor meeting. There was old rough cut benches to sit on, and I got splinters in my backside. But anyhow, we all stood up to sing a hymn and the big fat sister in front of me stood, too. That's when I noticed that about a half yard of material from that dress was stuck between her cheeks. I figgered that must be uncomfortable and so being a good boy, I reached up and pulled it out. She whirled around and gave me a black eye. Never said a word, just swung and hit me. Well sir, still trying to do the right thing, I kinda figgered that was the way it was supposed to be, so I tucked it back in.

"That's when she got the other eye. She knocked me flat on my back, and some of them church folks thought I was in the spirit and commenced to praying with me. Granddaddy was mad, but I heard him laughing about it later that night." The group roared with laughter.

Then someone heard a bellowing laugh coming from behind the speaker. One of the men recognized Thomas and immediately jumped to his feet. "Ten-hut!" he shouted.

"As you were, men," said the Major as he walked away snickering, "Tucked it back in..." Thomas walked back to his tent and picked up his bedroll.

"Bonner," he said, "we'll be leaving at dawn. You stay right here in front of this tent and look after your mistress. She don't make it home safely, I'm gonna whup all the hide off of you! Understand?"

"Yassuh, mister Major, suh. I sho nuff understand dat! Miss Caroline will be jis fine!"

Thomas unrolled his bed close to the nearest campfire and was asleep immediately.

Bonner lay quietly, listening to the soft snoring of Caroline inside the tent. "Lawd," he prayed, "keep these, your children, safe and sound through dis war. Amen."

Chapter sixteen

Dawn found Bonner loading the buggy with Caroline's luggage. Watching as two young men took down the tent, he whispered to Caroline, "Those boys ought to be home helping their paw. My two youngest are their age."

Caroline looked up. "They are at home," she said. "That's the Harrison twins. See that big, red-haired burly man over there, saddling his horse? Well, that's their paw, and according to Father, they were almost born side-saddle."

Bonner looked at the young men again. "Well what's you knows about that! The last time I sees those whelps is when they brought an old jersey cow up to your father's barn, wondering if he might save the old thing. Yes ma'am, I bet your poppa done delivered most of dem fellows what's following the Major," Bonner mumbled.

Caroline walked to Thomas as he stood drinking coffee. She nudged up close to his side. "Penny for your thoughts," she whispered.

"Would you settle for some hot coffee instead?" Thomas replied. The morning air had a touch of coolness for June. "Have Bonner to take the Cedar Creek road home; it'll take you through Davenport country. Silas Davenport will be the first place you come to. They will make you welcome. You can rest and sleep over there before going home," Thomas said.

Looking up at him, she replied, "Yes, sir! Any more orders, Major, before you ride off to your glorious adventures?"

"Huh-uh. Can I get a kiss?" he asked. As the couple embraced, some of the men cleared their throats loudly, while some whistled.

The first sergeant bellowed, "That'll be enough of that! Eyes front!"

As Thomas wiped her tears away, he said, "Stay safe. You and Bonner watch out for yourselves."

They had never told him of their incident while coming back from the railhead. "Yep. You do the same," she sniffed.

With a wide grin, he said, "I can see that Henry's 'yep' has done wore off on you." Thomas knew they would never make it to Brandy Station by the tenth, but little did he know they would make it in time to help in clearing out the Shenandoah Valley of Milroy's troops.

Caroline and Bonner watched from the buggy as Thomas and his men rode out of sight. In her mind, she had visualized a June wedding, but being practical as she was, it would come soon enough, she thought. "Let's go home, Bonner. I bet Mama Bonner and the children will want to see you," she remarked.

"Dat's where we're heading! Carter Town, here we come," Bonner replied. Cedar Creek trail was very narrow in places, bordered by dense forest on one side and a creek on the other. It kept the two swatting mosquitoes. It was a relief when they got to higher ground. Glancing at Caroline with a big grin, Bonner said, "You look like you did when you was a little girl. With dem measles all over yo' face."

"I don't believe I have a drop of blood left in my body. Thomas, you wait until I get my hands on you!" Caroline grumbled.

Laughing, Bonner said, "Yes ma'am. I'd bet he'd like that just fine; yes sir, just fine."

When they reached the Davenport farm, a haggard-looking woman came out of a log hut and stood at the fence. "Would this be Silas Davenport's place?" Caroline asked.

The old woman walked around the buggy and spat out tobacco juice. "Who in blazes might you be?" she demanded. Before Caroline could answer, the woman asked, "Is this here yore nigger, and how much you want fer him?"

Bonner looked at Caroline with a blank stare. Caroline had to do it. "Yep, how much you willing to pay for him?" she asked. It was all Caroline could do to barely hold her laughter.

The old woman walked around the buggy once more and shouted, "Get out of the buggy, nigger, and let me see how tall you are."

"Miss Caroline, what is yew doing?"

"Looks like the measles. Is that what you said?" whispered Caroline.

Greater Love Hath No Man

"Oh, Miss Caroline, you knows that old Bonner didn't mean nothing by that." He got out of the buggy and watched the old woman as she walked around looking him up one side and down the other as though he was on an auction block.

"Open up you mouth, nigger! I want to see how old you are!"

Caroline began laughing. She couldn't keep the joke going any longer.

"He's not for sale at any price! He's a free man," Caroline said.

The old woman walked back to the fence saying, "Huh! I think he's too old, anyway."

Bonner, realizing he had been fooled, stood quietly, grinning.

"Ma'am, you never did answer my question," said Caroline. "Is this Silas Davenport's place?"

Pointing toward a big log house, the old woman said, "Up there. That's my son's house, but he ain't home. . He left this morning going to his cousin Luther's place. Sarah and the kids are there."

When Bonner stopped the buggy in front of Silas' log home, a woman carrying a small child on her hip stood at the door. Caroline got out and walked to her. "Are you Sarah?" She asked.

"Who might you be?" Sarah said.

"I'm Caroline Glass from over Carter Town way," she answered.

"Caroline, I didn't recognize you! Don't you remember me? I'm Sarah. Used to be Sarah Jacobs. We went to school together when we were kids, remember?"

Caroline's face lit up. "Sarah Jacobs? Yes, I remember you. Girl, I wouldn't have recognized you in a hundred years." she said.

While the two women talked of old times, Bonner stretched out in the buggy, waiting on orders. He wasn't about to chance another one of Caroline's jokes. He was almost asleep when he heard Caroline calling his name.

"Bonner, leave my things on the porch, and drive the buggy around to the barn. It's all right. Nobody is gonna bother you. Stay with the animals tonight, and we'll get an early start in the morning. Don't worry, I'll bring you some supper."

The reunion was rudely interrupted when Silas came home. In fear, Sarah remained silent. He was a hard-spirited man, full of hate for man and beast. Caroline prepared herself for the worst.

"Where's my supper?" he grumbled. Sarah tried introducing Caroline. "Never mind about all that. Her nigger in the barn done told me who she is. Just fetch my supper!" he growled.

Caroline felt like a bug in a jar as she watched him gulp his food. Poor Sarah, she thought. Many young men were around when they were growing up. Why on earth would she settle for the likes of him?

"Get your things, and I'll show you where you can sleep," Sarah whispered to Caroline. Once in the bedroom, Sarah said, "He wasn't always like this. When we first married, we got along just fine. I was never happier."

"What on earth could have possibly happened to make him like that?" Caroline asked.

"The settlement and this blasted war. As long as we live here around his people, he's this way. Even the kids are scared of him; they run and hide when they see him coming," Sarah cried.

"Why don't you pack up the kids and move back to Carter Town and get out of this hell hole?" Caroline asked.

"Lord knows I've thought about it so many times, but where would I go? All my folks are dead, and the only brother I have is somewhere off with Robert E. Lee, fighting. God only knows, he might be dead too," she moaned.

Caroline embraced her. "If ever you get where you don't want to take it anymore, just pack your stuff up, and you and the kids come to the Glass house. We'll find a place for you, I promise. You hear?" Caroline said.

Sarah wiped tears from her eyes on her dress sleeve. "You hear?" Caroline asked again.

Sarah forced a smile and said, "I hear."

When the morning light came, Bonner was at the door, waiting. As they traveled, hardly a word was spoken. "Miss Caroline, are you feeling poorly?" Bonner asked. Caroline kept staring ahead silently. Bonner would hum different tunes, trying to get her to join in, but she paid no attention.

Finally, Caroline asked, "Bonner, do black men abuse their women?"

Bonner didn't know how to answer. "What you mean, child?"

"I'm not talking about you and Mama Bonner. I know how things are with y'all. But other men and their wives. Do they make slaves out of their women and talk ugly to them?" She asked.

"Child, I don't know what you mean. They already slaves," Bonner said.

"Never mind," she said. She leaned her head back and tried to sleep. Bonner began to worry about her. The bumps in the road told Bonner she wasn't sleeping, and it would just be a matter of time before she would tell him what was bothering her.

The trail they were traveling intersected with a cross road that led to the pike. Remembering Thomas' orders, Bonner stayed on the back trail.

Caroline said, "We could make better time if we hit the pike and turned off onto the Carter Town road." Bonner paid no attention but kept the buggy on the Cedar Creek trail. "Bonner, did you hear me? I said we could make better time."

Bonner interrupted, "I heard you, but I also heard what the Major said, too."

"Who owns this buggy?" she asked.

"The doctor do. He just lets us use it," Bonner said, smiling.

Caroline almost burst out laughing, "You're right, Bonner. I'm sorry. I don't know what's the matter with me," she said.

"Oh, that's all right, Miss Caroline, I knows you be troubled about your friend back there, and you know they sure ain't the nicest folks I ever met," Bonner answered.

Gunshots erupted over on the pike. Bonner stopped the team and listened. "Those shots are coming from where we would have been about now had we gone that way," he said.

Caroline was glad that Bonner refused to listen to her nagging, but she wasn't about to show it. "Probably someone hunting. Drive on," she ordered.

Bonner knew better than that but never gave a hint. "Yes, if we gonna make it before dark, we better get this here buggy on down the road," he remarked.

The sound of the shots faded away as they moved out of hearing distance. Neither one spoke another word until reaching the edge of town.

Standing in her yard, Maw Carter watched as they passed her house. A few townspeople greeted them as they drove along main street. There would be excitement at the Glass house tonight. When one of Bonner's sons saw them coming, he ran into the wash house shouting, "Mama, Mama, here comes Poppa and Miss Caroline up the road with dem horses in a full gallop!" Mama Bonner looked for herself.

"You run and tell the doctor that Miss Caroline is coming up the road, and tell your sisters to start drawing some bath water. We gonna have a time tonight."

Greater Love Hath No Man

Word of their return spread like wild fire throughout the community. Dr. Glass was the first to greet the two as they rode into the yard. "I didn't expect you back so soon. Did you run into any trouble?" he asked.

Caroline embraced her father and said, "It's a long story. I'll share it with you over supper, if that's all right."

Bonner waited patiently for the two to finish their conversation before driving the buggy to the stable.

When John Carter heard of their return, he had been busy stacking freshly cut wood. "If yew going to the shindig at the Glass house, you might get a move on!" Maw Carter said.

John hurried with a swat-off bath and change of clothes. Many things ran through his mind about Caroline's early return. He knew something was wrong. Richmond was too far for those two to be back this soon. As John was about to start his ride to the Glass house, he watched a coach being pulled by four black horses travel down the main road. Thinking aloud, he said, "I wonder who that important person might be? Well, guess it don't matter. Looks like we're heading to same place anyway."

Chapter seventeen

When the coach stopped outside the Glass home, a well-dressed lady stepped out, assisted by her driver. Some of the early arrivals watched as she entered the hallway. John Carter had followed the coach all the way.

He knew she wasn't from around here, and it was odd that her driver was white. Even though he was well-dressed, John couldn't help noticing how young he looked. Knocking the ash from his pipe, John walked to where he stood.

In a soft voice, he asked "Don't I know you?" The young driver shook his head. He could see the young man wasn't about to carry on a conversation, so he walked away, still glancing at him as though some mysterious power had drawn them together.

The town smithy stopped John long enough to remark, "What you think about that driver? Bet he's not a day over sixteen. What you think, John?"

John looked back at him one more time. "Yep, I think you hit the nail right on the head."

Dr. Glass was the first to see the well-dressed lady, and being a good host, he walked to her and introduced himself.

She said, "Why uncle, you don't recognize me? I'm Rosemary, your favorite niece."

"Rosemary, my love! Please forgive me. I'm so sorry I didn't recognize you. It's just been so long," he said as he embraced her.

"Looks like I got here just in time. What's the big occasion?" she asked.

"Oh, it's not any great occasion. Your cousin Caroline has just returned from a trip, and some of the townsfolk like to get together to celebrate her safe return," he answered.

Escorting her to a group of people, he announced, "May I have your attention please! This beautiful young lady is my niece, Miss Rosemary Glass from Mineral Wells. She has just arrived, and I want you make her welcome."

As the people gathered around trying to make conversation, the music began playing. It was hard to talk above the sound.

John Carter watched as she mingled among the people. Seated out in the coach was the young driver, listening to songs that brought back memories of his home. Arkansas was a long way from here, and Arkie was starting to feel the tug of homesickness. John Carter mingled with several people while waiting for the guest of honor. He couldn't get the young driver off his mind.

He walked outside to the coach and found Arkie sleeping. John hit the side of the door with his fist. The lad jumped up and almost hit his head on the top of the buggy.

"Were you asleep?" John asked.

"Just about," Arkie replied.

"They are about to serve some vittles inside. Thought you might like a bite to eat," John said.

"Now, that's sound good to me, but Miss Rosemary ain't let me know what she wants me to do just yet."

John knew that the lad wouldn't budge until she told him to. "Why don't I just fetch you some until you're told what to do about things? What you say about that?"

"Sounds good to me, mister," he answered.

"John Carter is the name. What might yours be?"

As they shook hands, the boy answered, "They call me Arkie. Glad to know you."

John liked this boy. "Just sit tight, Arkie. I'll bring you something to eat," he said. When John walked back into the house, he stopped one of Bonner's children and asked, "You see that white fellow out there near the coach that the white lady came driving up in?"

"Yassuh," the child nodded.

"Well, Miss Caroline wants you to fetch him something to eat, and do it now." The Bonner child skipped off to the kitchen humming Camptown Races.

Everyone was eating and drinking when John walked into the entertainment room. He noticed people having a good time, but he didn't see the guest of honor or the cousin from Mineral Wells.

John knew something was going on behind closed doors, and he was just about to find out. He walked to the doctor's study, thinking he might overhear a conversation, when Caroline came walking out.

"There you are. I've been looking all over for you. You're needed." John didn't know what to expect.

Slowly he followed Caroline back into the doctor's study. Dr. Glass said, "John, this is my niece, Rosemary Glass, from Mineral Wells. She has brought us a bit of bad news, I'm afraid."

"Oh, what sort of bad news?" John asked.

"I'll let her explain her story to you," the doctor said.

Rosemary smiled at John and began, "Three days ago, some Federal troops came to the home of my best friend and ordered all of them outside to watch them burn down their home and barn. They killed most all of the livestock and set fire to the crops, destroying it as well. They took my friend's husband off to some prison, and if it wasn't for that young boy out there on my coach, no telling what they would have done to her and their two little girls."

John asked, "What did the lad do to save the women folk?"

"They have a grinder in a old stone house run by a water wheel on a creek in back of their place. They grind meal for all the neighbors each year, and…"

"Hold it right there!" interrupted John. "you wouldn't be talking about Henry Watkins and his family, would you?"

"Precisely," she responded.

"Is Henry's family well and out of danger?" John asked.

"They are unharmed and staying in my home, for now," Rosemary answered.

John knew that Arkie should be in the room with them. "That lad out there; where does he fit into this picture?"

Caroline walked to the door and summoned Bonner. "Go fetch that young man that drove Rosemary here," she ordered

"Yes ma'am! I'll go now," he replied.

While Bonner was gone, Rosemary continued with the details. When she finished, she asked John, "You seem to know who I'm speaking of, isn't that right?"

"Yes ma'am. Henry was here just last month, and we got to know one another real well. Would you, by chance, know where they have taken him?" John asked.

"That's why I'm here Mr. Carter, seeking help," she replied.

John remained silent as he watched Caroline and her father talking. In his thoughts, he began to feel sorry for Henry.

A hush came over the room when Arkie walked in. "Come over here, Arkie," Rosemary said. The lad walked to her, obediently.

"This is Little Arkansas. His friends call him Arkie. Isn't that right?" Rosemary said and smiled at the boy.

The boy was embarrassed. Caroline tried to save him from all the questions by asking, "Have you had anything to eat?"

"Yes ma'am," he said.

"John, would you be so kind to have Bonner take Rosemary's coach to the barn, to feed and water her horses, and also have him to bring her things in and put them in the center guest room, if you don't mind. She will be staying the night."

John did as he was asked, but he first told Arkie he wanted to chat with him when he got back.

Doctor Glass excused himself, leaving the women to talk to one another. Rosemary didn't know about Caroline and Thomas.

"Tell me cousin, what's going on in your life besides helping your father in his practice? Will you be going to medical school when this war is over?" Caroline asked.

Rosemary expressed her gratitude for her hospitality and replied, "This war has kept me from doing a lot of things. Medical school is second on my list. I have been hoping that a certain young man would stop galloping around the countryside and settle down and ask me to marry him."

"Why, I think that's wonderful! I wasn't sure you would ever marry again," Caroline answered.

John Carter came back into the room. "I think the party is about to break up. Some of the guests were hoping to speak with you before they left, Miss Caroline." Caroline excused herself and walked out the door.

"Miss Rosemary, I was in hopes I could talk with you and Arkie about what happened," John said.

"There is very little I could add that you haven't already heard," she answered.

"What were these Federals wearing? I mean, did they carry a flag or any insignia of what unit they were with?" John asked.

"They were West Virginia Cavalry, led by a Major named Simmons," answered Arkie.

"Simmons? Are you sure?" John asked.

"I'm positive!" Arkie responded. "When they started setting fire to the house, Mrs. Watkins and her two girls ran out the back door. I was coming out of the barn, and one of the troopers shot at me. Missed my head by inches. The bullet hit a fence post, and I fell to the ground and played dead for a few minutes until he rode off.

"When he left and started shooting the pigs, I got Mrs. Watkins and her girls. We ran to the creek and hid in the mill. They never followed us. Seemed like all they wanted to do was get Mr. Watkins and burn his place."

John stood scratching his head. "Simmons... what did this Simmons look like? Did you get a good look at him?"

"Not really. I heard one of the troopers tell another that Major Simmons wanted Mr. Watkins on his big gray when he hanged him. After that I'm not sure."

"So you don't know whether or not they hanged him?" John asked.

"No, sir. They didn't hang him then. I rode into town and got Miss Rosemary as Mrs. Watkins asked me to, and she found out they had taken Mr. Watkins to a prison somewhere in Washington; we ain't sure where. That's why we came here, in hopes that Miss Caroline could find out."

John paced the floor, and scratched his head. "Tell you what we are going to do," John began.

Rosemary interrupted, "Before we start trying to do anything, let's wait until Caroline has a chance to tell us what she is going to do."

Bonner entered the room then, carrying a tray of several drinks. "The doctor has sent you some refreshments," he said. Rosemary was served first and then John. When he got to Arkie, he said, "You too young for this here stuff; I'll fetch you some water."

"Bonner, let that young man have one! It'll be all right. He's well deserved it," scolded Rosemary.

Bonner smiled. "Yes ma'am! I'll do just that."

While the three sat waiting for Caroline, Rosemary leaned her head against the back of the chair, almost drifting off to sleep. Before Bonner left the room, John caught his attention and motioned for him to look in Rosemary's direction. He could see she was exhausted. "I'll fetch Miss Caroline," he whispered

"Would you like to go to your room and rest?" John whispered to Rosemary. She remained silent with her eyes shut.

Speaking to Arkie, John said, "Looks like it's just you and me, partner."

Greater Love Hath No Man

With the guests gone, Caroline returned to the room to find Rosemary sound asleep.

John put his finger over his lips. "Shush," he whispered.

Caroline smiled and whispered, "She is worn out. I should have seen her to her room before I left."

John motioned for Arkie to follow him out of the room and down the hall while Caroline roused Rosemary. "Partner, why don't you think about staying over at my place tonight, while the ladies decide on what to do," John suggested.

Meanwhile, Caroline shook Rosemary, saying, "Let me show you to your room; we can talk about this later."

"How embarrassing! Has everyone left? Where's Arkie?" she asked.

"Never mind about all that for now. He went home with John Carter. Let's get you up to bed. You're exhausted," Caroline said.

Chapter eighteen

The next morning at breakfast Rosemary apologized once again for dozing in the presence of Caroline's company.

Caroline was concerned about Henry. She knew looking for him would be like looking for a needle in a haystack, especially now that Simmons was back in the picture.

"I know it was too late for you to see how our town is being built back, but maybe before you leave you can get a first hand view of what our beloved Major Simmons did before help arrived," Caroline said.

Greater Love Hath No Man

Bonner held his breath while he served the two ladies. He knew that any minute now, a certain Confederate Major might get mentioned, and he didn't want any part of that. He was delighted when Caroline said, "Bonner, I need you to take a message to the railhead and see that it's sent. As usual, don't come home until you get an answer, no matter how long it takes! Understood?"

"Yes, ma'am. It'll be a pleasure," he said with relief.

"Get me pen and paper, so I can write this message." When she finished and Bonner had left the room, Caroline said, "Cousin, I hope you are prepared to stay awhile. This may take a day or two."

The railhead was forty miles from Carter Town and under Federal control. Bonner was no stranger to carrying messages for Caroline, but this time it would be different.

The rugged terrain of mining country was where people called mountaineers lived. They didn't like it much when strangers rode in sight of their dwellings. A black man riding a mule and carrying a shotgun who was about to ride close could definitely spark things in action.

Another consideration was that once reaching the railhead, there would be hundreds of Federals camped near and around the depot. In fact, the telegrapher himself would probably be a Federal solider, posing another threat. He would have to be very sly. But old Bonner was no fool. He had many years experience of playing dumb.

The sun was starting to rise above the hill when Bonner walked to the barn. Hezekiah, his son, had saddled his favorite mule. Hezekiah handed him the shotgun and asked, "Poppa, you ever had to use this here thing?"

"Why you ask such foolish questions like that? You'd know it if'n I had. Go get yo' chores done. I'll be back in a few days," Bonner answered.

The boy watched as his father rode down the hill and out of sight.

While the Glass family was rousing from their slumber, an old Dominick rooster sounded its famous wake up call. The smell of bacon cooking in the kitchen filled the air. It was a beautiful morning, and with birds singing and teaching their young to fly, it seemed to assure everything was in order.

With Bonner gone, Mama Bonner and her girls had to look after things for Caroline. "Good morning," Mama Bonner said as she walked into Rosemary's room.

With one eye open, Rosemary replied, "Morning. What time is it?" she asked.

"Da sun is up and the good Lawd has done give us a pretty day to be glad we is alive," Mama Bonner said. Pouring water from the pitcher and into the bowl, she asked, "You coming down for your breakfast, or should I bring it to you?"

"I'll be down shortly, after I dress," Rosemary replied.

"Want me to stay and help you?" Mama Bonner asked.

"No; that won't be necessary. I'll be down, later," she answered.

In the Carter's house, at the edge of town, Maw Carter prepared a breakfast fit for a king: hot biscuits covered with fresh churned butter and topped with wild honey made Arkie gorge like he was starved. It pleased John to see him eat like that.

"Gonna be a fine day," John remarked, before walking outside to the wood pile.

"Where's he going?" Arkie asked.

"You just eat your food, and don't worry about John. He's a fixin' to fill up the wood box," Maw said.

"Ain't he gonna eat?" Arkie asked.

"He done ate before you got up," she answered.

Greater Love Hath No Man

John brought an armload of wood in and dropped it into the wood box. Brushing off his arms, he said, "Think I'll sit down and have a cup of coffee with you, partner."

As the two sat quietly drinking coffee, the dogs started barking at someone riding up.

Maw Carter went to the door and watched as a man dismounted and walked to the porch. Waiting for the knock, she hesitated before opening the door. "Want me to open it?" she shouted to John. John walked to the door and greeted the stranger himself.

"I'm Ben Fields from over near the Davenports. I was asked to come and give you a message," said the visitor.

"Come in, Fields, and we can talk it over with a cup of coffee," John answered. Maw poured Fields a cup of coffee as the two men sat down at the table.

"Fields, meet my young friend Arkie from Arkansas; Arkie, meet Ben Fields. Seems he has a message fer me," John said

"Want that I should leave?" Arkie asked.

"Stay put," John said.

Fields began to explain, "Yesterday evening, about a hundred or so Yankee cavalry came riding down on the Davenports, burning and killing like a bunch of border ruffians. They didn't get the job done much before the Davenports cut them to pieces. Trapped them in a holler, that's what they done! Old man Davenport danced around waving his hat, shouting, 'Pour it to them boys'."

"How many did the Davenports lose?" John asked.

"Well, too many. They killed Silas and burned his place, after they killed his mother. The old man said she brought it on her self, trying to run them off with a load of birdshot. You know, I think the war done drove that old man crazy. That's what I come to tell you. He thinks Carter Town might get it, again, so he sent me to warn you."

"You wouldn't by chance know what outfit they were, would you?" John asked.

"The old man seems to think it was the same bunch that burned y'all out before, but who knows? They probably some more of that bunch they tangled with last month, if you asking me, but who cares, anyway? They all just murdering Yankees to me."

"Which way you going when you leave here?" John asked.

"Through the hills. Too many Yanks on the pike," he answered.

"I wonder if you will take a message to a fellow up in mine country fer me?" John asked.

Thinking about John's question for a minute, Fields said, "You thinking the old man might be right, don't you?"

"Maybe," John responded.

"Who is this fellow, and whereabouts can I locate him?" Fields asked.

"Snickers Gap is where you'll find him, and his name is…"

"Hold it right there! I ain't going up to no Snickers Gap and get my head shot off! I'll take my chances with the Yanks! No thank you!" Fields interrupted.

When he left, John and Arkie walked outside to the barn. "What you gonna do?" Arkie asked.

"Not sure," he replied. "but we just can't sit here doing nothing, now can we?" John asked. With Thomas off somewhere in the Shenandoah, chasing Yankees, leaving mostly old men to fight, John began to worry. Trying not showing his concern, he asked, "Partner, how would you like to take a ride up in the mountains with me?"

"What about Miss Rosemary? What if she needs me?" he questioned.

"We'll stop on the way and let her know, but don't say a word about what Fields told us, understood?"

Greater Love Hath No Man

When the two left the Glass home, they traveled the same trail that Bonner had taken just three hours previously.

It was narrow and hazardous, and in places the ride slowed to a walk. When they reached the top of one of the mountains, Arkie looked out across the valley below and asked, "Where's all that smoke coming from over there in that valley?"

"What smoke?" John asked.

Pointing toward an area that belched out smoke from the ground, Arkie said, "There! Right over there!"

"Those are hot springs. We'll come back that way and take a bath, if you care to," John answered.

"Are they safe?" Arkie asked.

"Oh, yeah. I've taken lots before. Makes a man feel good," John replied.

"My maw told me about how she and her family used to do that when she was a little girl, over in our state," Arkie answered.

"We getting near where we're going, so it's best we keep shut for awhile," John said. When they reached a slope that ran down into a dell, they could hear people talking. John dismounted, handing Arkie his horses reigns. "Stay here until I get back. I'm gonna see what this is all about," John whispered.

He could see two mountaineers arguing over something, but he was too far away to understand what it was. He eased a little closer and saw Bonner tied and lying on the ground. They were arguing over who would get the mule. John recognized both of the men.

Aiming his rifle at the two, he said, "What you doing with my nigger?" When they saw John had the advantage, they immediately began apologizing.

"Well, John Carter, we didn't know! All that darkie kept saying was that he's a Glass nigger."

Arkie heard all the loud talk and walked up behind John. "Untie Bonner for me, while I talk to these fine gentlemen of the hills," John ordered.

Pulling out his Arkansas toothpick, Arkie made one slice at the ropes, freeing Bonner's hands.

"Thank you, master Arkie! Am I glad to see you!" Bonner cried with relief.

While Bonner and Arkie were having their conversation, John took the two men aside and began a discussion with them. A few minutes later they came back laughing as though nothing had happened.

"Bonner, you're free to go on about your business now," John said. "Arkie, we're through here. Are you in the mood for one of those hot baths your Mama told ya about?'

With a grin, Arkie nodded his head. As the two rode toward the springs, Arkie asked, "You think old Bonner will be all right?"

"Bonner's chances are better with those boys in blue than what he just went through. But to answer your question, yeah he'll be just fine."

At the Glass home, another situation was taking place. Dr. Glass had been summoned to the Garland home to deliver a baby. While he was getting things in order, Rosemary volunteered to assist him. Dr. Glass knew she was more than qualified. "It'll be a pleasure having you along. I was hoping to speak to you about something, anyway," he said.

As the two rode away, Caroline stood silently, watching as the buggy drove out of sight. Mama Bonner came walking toward her, saying, "Child, everything is gonna be all right. Your Thomas is a coming home and gonna sweep you off your feet like a broom. You just wait and see. You hear?"

"I hope so. Yes, I really hope so," she said.

Greater Love Hath No Man

Sidney Garland and three small children stood on the porch waiting as Dr. Glass and Rosemary got out of the buggy and went inside. An hour later, Rosemary walked out, carrying a newborn wrapped in a blanket. "Mr. Garland, say hello to your new daughter."

Sidney Garland danced around with so much excitement he almost tore the porch down. "Yee ha, yee ha," he shouted over and over.

"Don't you want to hold her?" Rosemary asked.

"Not me! No sir; I might break her," he replied.

Dr. Glass walked out on the porch and said, "Your wife is fine, but she might want to stay in bed a couple of days before she hangs out a wash."

"Uncle, why don't I stay, and someone can come get me tomorrow. I believe she could use the help," Rosemary offered.

"Suit yourself. I'll have Caroline drive out and get you tomorrow," he answered.

Chapter nineteen

Early morning brought Rosemary outside with a load of bedclothes to be washed. She had already built a fire under the iron washtub by the time Caroline arrived. With piles of clothing waiting to be boiled, a helping hand would definitely be appreciated. Hesitating for a few minutes before getting out of the buggy, Caroline watched as Rosemary separated several garments from each other.

"Looks like you got your hands full. Let me give you a hand," Caroline offered.

Rosemary blew a strand of hair from her face and grunted, "All help is welcome."

Greater Love Hath No Man

Caroline lifted a pair of long-johns from out of the washtub with the stirring stick. Holding onto the underwear, each woman twisted until the garment was drained of water. They continued the chore for over an hour. Finally Rosemary said, "We need to take a break."

When the women looked at each other and saw how wet and ragged each looked, they began laughing. "How is the new Garland and her mother?" Caroline asked.

"Oh, they're fine. It's old man Garland that'll have the problems," Rosemary said.

"Why is that?" Caroline asked.

"Look at him over there on the porch. Slept out here all night, drunker than a coot."

"Yep, and I bet he's got a crick in his neck," Caroline said.

"He needs a crick in something else if you ask me," Rosemary laughed.

It was evening before the ladies finished. Leaving several lines of clothing hanging out to dry, they drove away. Rosemary said, "You know all that work back there? We must have not done so good."

"Why is that?" Caroline asked.

"Well, you see those rain clouds banking? Looks like the man upstairs thinks our wash needs a better rinse," Rosemary answered.

When the buggy stopped in front of the Glass home, Hezekiah was there to greet them.

"I'll take it to the barn before you ladies gets wet," he said.

With a grin, Caroline thanked him, and the two walked inside. "Phew! We made it just in time. A few minutes more and we'd got our bath the hard way," Rosemary said.

Mama Bonner came walking down the hallway. "Miss Caroline, child, just look at you! Just look at the both of you! Y'all look like you been in the hog pen!"

"You're right, Mama Bonner; we have been, but a different kind of sty," Caroline said.

Looking puzzled, Mama Bonner asked Rosemary, "What's she mean different kind of sty?"

"Never mind, Mama. Right now, we both could stand a good hot bath," Caroline answered.

The storm brought high winds and rain. At times lightning would flash across the sky, lighting up the heavens. Two lamps burned brightly on Dr. Glass' desk as he sat reading. New methods had been found in treating different diseases, and he was anxious to share his findings with Rosemary.

A late meal was prepared for the ladies, so Mama Bonner knocked on the doctor's door. There was no answer, so she gently knocked once more. Mama Bonner peeked in and saw the old gent with his head down on the desk, sound asleep.

She walked quietly out of the room carrying one of the lamps, holding it high as she moved down the hall.

In the kitchen Caroline and Rosemary sat at a small table eating and talking. Mama Bonner said, "The good doctor has done read himself to sleep, again."

"I'll wake him and put him to bed when I'm finished," Caroline answered. She hurried with her meal.

When Caroline left the room, Rosemary asked Mama Bonner, "You missing Poppa Bonner, aren't you?"

She hesitated before answering, "Child you sho' do know what to say."

The storm was continuing with its high winds. At times, sheets of rain hit the structures, making it sound as thought it was tearing boards loose.

Carter Town was in the middle of a tornado but fortunately, with the river on one side and mountains on the other, it passed over, hitting the mountainside. When daylight came, all sorts of debris lay on the ground, from tree limbs to wrecked buildings.

Greater Love Hath No Man

Rosemary woke up early and walked outside to see what damage had been done to the flower garden. Her father and uncle had a lot in common when it came to horticulture. Each had a green thumb and prize winning roses. Rhododendrons were blooming all over the countryside, along with other wild flowers. This made roses quite an issue among many people, including Mary Todd Lincoln.

Rosemary walked to the front of the house as John Carter rode up. "Good morning Mr. Carter," she greeted politely.

"Morning. Is the doc home?" he asked.

"Yes, he is. Go on inside; you'll probably find him in his study. Is there something wrong?" She asked.

"It's Maw Carter. I'm afraid we might be losing her," John explained.

Rosemary followed him inside and went to the kitchen to find Mama Bonner. Hezekiah was walking out the back door with a bucket of scraps for the hogs when Rosemary saw him. "Go hitch up the buggy, and hurry!" She shouted. Hearing the urgency in her voice, he put the bucket down and ran to the barn.

The hooves of John's horses pounded loudly as he rode at a full gallop back toward his home.

The town smithy stopped his hammering when John rode past his shop. He knew something was happening. He pulled off his apron and gave it a toss. He saddled his horse and rode to Maw Carter's. By the time he got there, several people had gathered and were standing in the yard.

Arkie sat in a porch swing watching, as half the town assembled. When Dr. Glass arrived with Rosemary, everyone stepped aside, making way for them to pass.

The crowd patiently waited for word from the doctor or Rosemary. Maw Carter had been a widow for several years, and John was her only child. She helped rear

John's two boys after his wife died and during his adventurous life among the Indians.

Dr. Glass walked out of the house about an hour later. "Folks, Maw Carter went peacefully to be with our lord. My niece, Rosemary and some of the ladies are preparing her now for burial. You may see her after all that's done," he announced.

Several people left, returning to their homes and work, while others remained, hoping to see her once more before her burial.

John sat staring into space, thinking about the times as a small boy, how he and his father would come home from fishing, and how his mother was there, giving orders about bringing smelly fish into her kitchen. The Carters were the first to settle that area, so as folks started moving in, the settlement adopted the name of Carter Town. Losing his father at a young age to a sickness no one knew much about had caused him to admire her more and more, as she had struggled to keep food on the table.

She had been able to hunt and clean game as well as any man and had always kept a bountiful garden. She had made all the clothing they owned, including the uniforms her grandsons wore in the war. John's thoughts vanished the moment Rosemary laid her hand on his shoulder.

Patting her hand, he said, "Well, we come in this world knowing that in time we all must leave. It's just that it seems so soon."

"We're ready," came a voice from one of the ladies. John got up and walked into the front room where his mother's body lay, wearing a blue dress she had made just for this occasion.

John approached the body, and staring down at her, he whispered, "I wish the boys could be here, and we could bring back all the good times we had together. But I know those days are gone, so now I leave you, my good mother to rest in the arms of our lord. I'm sure you and Paw will have a lot of things to talk over." Wiping his eyes as he walked away, Arkie went to him. Without saying a word, he followed John everywhere he went.

At the back of the house, two men worked with hammers and saws to build a wooden casket. When Dr. Glass returned home, he told Caroline of Maw's death. She wasted no time in leaving, but as she walked out a large freight wagon, driven by a man and woman with three small children, drove up.

The wagon was loaded down with furniture and household goods. She couldn't tell who was in the wagon, which was blocking her way. Whoever it was had apparently come to stay. Caroline strained her eyes, trying to see. The woman was wearing a bonnet pulled down almost over her eyes. When Caroline stopped the buggy, the woman shouted, "Is that you, Caroline Glass?"

Caroline responded, "Yep! Now who in blue blazes are you?"

The woman removed her bonnet, and Caroline jumped out the buggy shouting, "Sarah! Sarah Jacobs! I mean Davenport!"

Sarah climbed down from the wagon, and the two women hugged each other happily. "Where are you heading, and who is this feller you got driving you?"

"Oh, this here is Dan Holland. He knows your father, and he's a good friend of John Carter."

"Speaking of John Carter, I was just heading to Maw Carter's place. She has just passed away, and most everyone is down there," Caroline said.

"I noticed a lot of people over near her place when we passed by, but I didn't know what was going on. So, she has just passed away, you say?" Dan asked.

"I'll back my buggy, so you can turn your wagon around, and we'll go down there," Caroline said. Soon they were all traveling in the same direction.

The yard was full of people when they got there. Folks were bringing all kinds of food and placing it on the three long boards that were joined together and resting on empty kegs with a tablecloth draped over the top for a table.

Some old men with long white beards sat around talking about old times and how they remembered some of the hard times that Maw had gone through.

When Dan Holland arrived, he went inside to pay his respects. He saw John standing near the back door talking to another man. Waiting to see whether John would notice him, he stood quietly, not wanting to disturb John's conversation with the other man. Finally, Dan interrupted, "Anyone know a feller named John Carter around here?" he asked.

They were delighted to see each other. They had a lot of things to talk about, but this wasn't the time.

"I'm sorry about Maw. Did she suffer?" Dan asked.

"No, Dan. The doc said she went peacefully," John answered. "You couldn't have heard about Maw's death this soon; what brings you here?" John asked.

"A big freight wagon and a woman and three kids," Dan answered.

"You done gone and got yourself hitched and had three pups? My, you're a fast worker," John said and then laughed.

"Naw, it ain't nothing like that. She's Silas Davenport's widow."

"Yeah, I heard about that. Well, what's gonna happen to them?" John asked.

"I don't know. She said that Caroline Glass had invited her and her children to come live here," Dan answered.

"Sounds like Caroline. I bet old Doc Glass will love that," John remarked.

Greater Love Hath No Man

As the two men talked, Rosemary walked by, catching Dan's undivided attention. "Whoa!" he said, "who might that be?"

"That, my friend, is Caroline's cousin from Mineral Wells, and she is out of your class. She's studying to be a doctor, and I might say she's a good one at that," John answered.

"Hmmm, doctor or no doctor, I still want to meet her. She ain't married, is she?" Dan asked.

"Widow, I hear, and not interested in anyone but one man, and I'm anxious to see just how that's going to come about," John answered.

The people were gathering in front of the house, ready to eat. Rosemary walked to where John stood talking with Dan.

"Mr. Carter, the people have asked if you would mind saying the blessing," Rosemary said.

There was never a better time for Dan Holland to introduce himself, but before he could say a word, Rosemary introduced herself to him.

Dan was caught completely off guard. He couldn't keep his eyes from hers. She stammered, "Th-they are calling everyone outside for the prayer. Shall we go?"

All Dan could say was, "Uh huh. Uh, yes'm."

His heart was beating like a drum. He had never felt like this before. If there were such a thing as love at first sight, this would surely be it.

Chapter twenty

Carter Town would miss Maw and her sternness, but as the poet says, "Life must go on."

Dan Holland tossed and turned all night thinking about the most beautiful woman he had ever met. Her jet black hair shined like the sun's rays bouncing off a crow's wing. At least that's what he told John most of the night. Arkie had heard enough. He had tried covering up his head a couple of times, but it had been of no use, so he snatched the blanket off his bed and grabbed his pillow. He had headed outside to the porch swing, when Dan asked, "Where you going?"

"Anywhere to get away from you and all that lovesick bellering," Arkie had grumbled.

"Now Arkie, don't you think she's the prettiest thing this side of heaven?" Dan had asked.

"Don't know. The last time I was there, I was too young to remember, but I do know one thing. I'm going to find a place where I can get some sleep and leave you dreaming about your black-haired beauty before she flies off with the crows!" Arkie responded.

"Be that way, then! The trouble with you is, you're too young to know about such things," Dan remarked.

"Well, if it makes me keep people up all night, talking about the same thing over and over, I hope I never learn," Arkie said on his way out the door. The sound of John's snoring told Dan that he was now alone in his conversation. Giving up the idea as talking to the wind, he drifted off to sleep.

The next morning, things got interesting. While the three were eating breakfast, someone knocked on the front door. It was Mr. Rivercomb. Arkie went to the door to greet him, while John continued eating. "Would John be here?" asked the visitor.

John could see who it was. "Come on in, Mr. Rivercomb," he called.

Mr. Rivercomb walked in. "I just came by to pay my respects and to tell you just how sorry I feel about your Maw. She was a fine woman, and I feel bad about not attending her funeral, but I've been sick myself. This is the first day I've felt like anything useful," he replied.

"She would understand. Won't you sit down and have some breakfast with us?" John asked

"Oh, no thanks. I just came by to pay my respects. Oh, by the way, the Yanks must be in this area somewhere," Rivercomb said.

"What makes you say that?" John asked.

"Well, when I crossed Grinder's Ridge, I looked down and saw what looked to be the whole Davenport family coming this way," he said.

Dan Holland dropped his fork in his plate. "Dang it! They're coming after Sarah, and they'll shoot me on sight if they see me!" Dan said.

John walked Rivercomb to the door, thanking him for coming. Dan sat at the table stewing over what he had just heard. He was drinking his coffee and staring into space as John sat down and finished his breakfast. Arkie sat quietly and watched as Dan fumbled with his meal. "What makes you think they got bad feelings about you Dan?" John asked.

"Because I drove Sarah and her young ones here," he answered.

"Well, you just did what you were asked. What harm is that?"

"John, you know that old man. He's *crazy*, I tell you! Even the whole damn Yankee cavalry is scared of him."

"I doubt that; but I tell you one thing, if you haven't done anything wrong, then there's no need to be concerned. But if you have, I'll be the first to hand you over to them," John said sternly.

"Sarah came begging me to drive her and the kids here, being what the Yanks did to Silas and his Maw. The old man got it in his head she was a Davenport, and she was to marry up with one of the other boys, so she came to me for help. I felt sorry for her, and I helped her load what we could on that old freight wagon. We left in the night. I'm just wondering who might have told them we were here," Dan replied.

"If that's all there is to it, I'll stand by you, but if there is something else you haven't told me about, I'll shoot you myself," John growled.

"Oh, John! You wouldn't shoot me, would you?" Dan asked.

Without answering, John walked out the back door to the barn. "Now, where do you suppose he's going?" Dan asked.

"Probably the same place I'm going; to the Glass house," Arkie answered.

Dan followed and saddled his mount. He was ready to ride the other direction when he saw the Davenport family coming down the main road. His heart was beating faster than a racehorse. Rosemary was nowhere in his thoughts. He had fought alongside this family and knew they meant business in everything they chose to do. Dan spurred his mount and rode full gallop toward Mineral Wells. He knew that once he reached Reverend Kelly's, it might be safer.

When the Davenports stopped out in front of the Glass house, Caroline greeted them. "What you want here?" Caroline asked.

The old man rode up to the porch while the others remained. "You got one of our'n in there, and we want her!" he shouted.

Dr. Glass heard the commotion and came to Caroline's side. "Here, here! What's this all about?" he asked.

"You got one of our'n in your house, and we want her and the children out here, right now!" the old man demanded.

Dr. Glass turned to Caroline."Go fetch Sarah and her children, before this gets out of hand."

Before Caroline walked inside, Sarah came out the door, shaking her finger at the old man, calling him an old coot and refusing to go back. Dr. Glass remained silent while the two argued. John Carter and Arkie rode up and dismounted.

Walking to the porch and standing by Dr. Glass, with his hand on his side arm, John said, "Davenport, you and I have been friends a long time. You might ought to go and settle this in a better way. We wouldn't want to end it right here and now, would we?"

"Carter, this is none of your affair. Yours or the Glass family. We wish no trouble out any of y'all," he said.

"Sarah and her children are guests in my home and may stay long as they like," argued Caroline.

Two more Davenports rode to the old man's side and drew their side arms. "What's the matter, Paw? They ain't gonna let her go?"

"Why don't y'all leave, and we can meet down by the river at the crossing and talk this over before somebody gets killed." cried Sarah.

The old man looked John in the eyes while answering Sarah, "Fifteen minutes. That's all; just fifteen minutes." The old man backed his horse and rode toward the river. His sons followed.

Sarah looked at Caroline with tears streaming down her face, as she said, "I'm sorry. I had no idea this would happen, or I would have never come here."

"You told me they were going to make you marry one of the other sons against your will, didn't you?" Caroline asked.

"They will," she answered. "but it's better than getting a lot of people killed. That old man out there is crazy, I tell you! He won't stop until I get in that wagon with all three of my children and get back to Davenport Holler!"

"Well, you're not going! Davenports or no Davenports, and that's final!" Caroline grumbled. Rosemary stood quietly, listening to every word.

Dr. Glass and John Carter walked inside to the study. "Fifteen minutes is ticking away. What do you think we should do?" he asked John.

"You know, doc, I mean no offense to the ladies, but sometimes they're more trouble than they're worth. Now you understand why I never remarried."

"Precisely," he answered.

Arkie came to the door and motioned for John to come. "They ain't gonna let her go," he said.

"Who ain't going to let her go?" John asked.

"Miss Caroline, that's who! She says she's gonna shoot the first Davenport that rides up."

"If this don't beat all! It's not enough to fight the Yanks, but you got to fight among yourselves as well. Where's she at now?" John asked.

"Outside, trying to talk Sarah into staying, but Sarah has done hitched up the mules to her wagon, and she's fixing to leave."

"Women! Who can figure what a woman might do next? Come on. Let's see if we can stop this before something happens!" John said, as they walked outside.

Sarah and her children were already boarded on the wagon when John and Arkie walked up. "Stop her, John! Oh, please, stop her!" cried Caroline.

"Miss Caroline, I can't stop her from doing what she wants to do," John answered.

"But that's just it! She doesn't want to go! Not really, do you Sarah?" Caroline pleaded.

"It's no use in all this, Caroline! I've made up my mind! I'm going back before someone gets killed on my account, and that's final!"

"Can't you do something, John?" sobbed Caroline.

"I'll ride out with her and talk on her part, but I'm not promising nothing! You hear?" he said.

John rode beside the wagon as they pulled out of the yard. Arkie stood beside Caroline and watched as they rode out of sight.

"Why don't you go with him, in case he needs you?" she asked. Rosemary stood by the door and heard everything.

Looking over at Rosemary, Arkie asked, "Would it be okay if I did that, ma'am?"

"That's strictly up to you, Arkie," she answered.

Arkie mounted his horse. "Thank you, ma'am," he said to Rosemary. He rode hard to catch up with the wagon. They topped a knoll that overlooked the river basin. Sarah could see the Davenports, lying on the ground, allowing their horses to graze. The old man still sat in his saddle, with one leg crossed over the horn, when they drove up.

Arkie walked his horse behind the wagon and dismounted while John stopped his mount in front of the old man. When the other Davenports saw what was happening, they all mounted and approached the wagon.

"We was just fixing to come and fetch you home, gal! It's a good thing you're here," the old man growled.

"I hate you old man and the whole lot of you. You know I'm not willing, but for the sake of avoiding bloodshed, I'll go," cried Sarah.

The old man ordered one of the boys to dismount and climb up on the wagon. Tying his horse to the tailgate and looking Arkie over as he got up on the wagon, he said, "Little boy, you better be careful with that big knife. You might cut off something you might want to use if'n yew ever get married." The Davenports thought that was funny. The young Davenport that sat down beside Sarah kissed her on the cheek.

Wiping her cheek with her hand, she said, "E-ew," disgustedly.

"You leave my Mama alone, Uncle Zed! Ye hear!" barked Sarah's oldest child.

John Carter watched and listened to everything that was happening. "What's next, Davenport?" he asked.

"What you mean, Carter?" the old man replied.

"When you get her home, what comes next?" John repeated.

"He's gonna make me marry this nitwit sitting here, that's what!" Sarah answered.

Standing up in the stirrups and aiming his pistol at the old man's head, John said, "Don't think so!" When Arkie saw what was happening, he prepared himself for a fight. All the other Davenports aimed their weapons at John, ready to fire.

The old man looked at John and said, "You mean you'd risk your life meddling in something that's not none of your affair?"

"Davenport, I'm doing exactly what you would do if you saw someone taken against their will. How many times have we seen that happen to our neighbors and loved ones here lately?" John said quietly.

"Yeah, but this here is different. This here is family," the old man argued.

"How you figure that, when we were all one big family until this war came? Now look at us, fighting one another, brother against brother; it don't make much sense, now does it?" John asked. "But those damn Yankees come telling us how we gonna live, and if we don't like it we can fight or leave, so we chose to fight."

When the old man saw John's point, he said, "Family, put your guns away. There's been enough killing. Sarah, I'm sorry you feel the way you do. I was in hope I could enjoy my grandchildren, but if you don't want to come back, I'll leave that decision up to you."

Sarah nudged Zed off the wagon and said, "I'll be living in Carter Town for awhile. You're welcome to come visit your grandchildren as long as you don't try and run their lives."

The old man dropped his head as he turned his mount and motioned for the rest of his family to leave.

Sarah waited until the dust settled as she watched her in-laws ride over the hill and out of sight. She turned the wagon around and began her journey back to Caroline's house.

The further into her ride the more she thought about all the rough talk and threats the old man made, but there was still a tenderness toward his grandchildren in his voice.

When she stopped the wagon in front of the house, Dora asked, "Are we going home, Mama?"

"You get in there wif your brother and stop asking questions." Sarah growled.

Greater Love Hath No Man

Chapter twenty-one

It was high noon when John and Arkie rode toward John Carter's home. Stopping by the graveyard, John dismounted and walked to his mother's grave. Removing his hat, he whispered words that Arkie didn't understand.

He watched as John knelt down and patted the grave before walking back to his mount.

John said, "You know we got to do something about all these acorns falling on the graves. Everywhere they fall an oak tree tries to come up. It won't be long before we'll be pulling up oak trees just to put flowers on our people's graves."

Greater Love Hath No Man

As the two rode away, John said, "Not that I don't like your company, but don't you think Rosemary could use a helping hand about now?"

Arkie smiled, "I know when a feller's not needed anymore."

John asked, "You like that bay you're riding?"

"Yeah. She's nice and gentle," Arkie answered.

"Well, keep her. She's yours. Stop by the house sometime, and I'll write you out a bill of sale," John said, smiling.

Arkie patted the side of his horse's neck and said, "I ain't never owned a horse before."

"Well, you do now," John said as he rode away.

Rosemary was in the flower garden when Arkie approached. She watched him dismount and walk the horse to where she was. "I see you made it back, all in one piece," she said happily.

"Yes'm. Wasn't a whole lot to it," Arkie said.

"Sarah explained what happened. I'm afraid I have a bit of bad news, though," she said.

Arkie stared at the ground. "What sort of bad news?" he asked hesitantly.

"Bonner is home, and I'm afraid we're back where we started. They have no earthly idea where Henry might be," she replied.

Without speaking, Arkie led his mount to the barn. He and Henry had developed a strong bond between them and the thought of never seeing his friend again brought tears to his eyes.

Rosemary knew the news would have an effect on the lad, so she began thinking of a plan that would give him hope.

She walked to the barn and found him grooming his horse. "My, that's a mighty fine bay you've been riding. It was nice of Mr. Carter to let you use her, while we've been here."

He turned to where she couldn't see his tears. "He gave her to me," he mumbled.

She knew this conversation would change his feelings for a few moments. "You mean he just up and *gave* her to you?"

He wiped away the tears with his shirt sleeve and turned. "Yes, ma'am. He said I should stop by his place, and he would write me out a bill of sale."

"How nice of Mr. Carter to do that. I bet she's at least a fifty dollar horse, or more. Wouldn't you say?" Rosemary asked.

"Oh, yes ma'am. I'd say more," Arkie beamed proudly.

She could see her plan was working. "I'm going back inside. Mama Bonner has fixed us something to eat. Are you about ready?" she asked.

"Yes ma'am. Just let me turn Molly out to pasture," he answered.

"Molly is her name?" Rosemary asked.

"Yes ma'am. That's the name I give her. John — I mean Mr. Carter — called her something else, but I like Molly better," he said.

"I think Molly is a pretty name. Sounds like it just might fit. Come along now, or your meal will get cold," Rosemary said. He closed the gate to the pasture, and the two walked to the house.

Over their meal, Rosemary said, "You know, we might ought to think about leaving in the morning. I bet Mildred and her girls are sick with worry."

Arkie continued eating as he nodded his head. Caroline came into the room looking for one of Sarah's children. They had a game of hide-and-seek going, and it was her turn to find them. Arkie saw the child, as he crouched behind some barrels. As Caroline got close to the

183

barrels, Arkie would say, "You're getting warmer." The little boy would stick his head around the barrel with his finger pressed to his lips to shush Arkie. When Caroline did find him, they both began to laugh.

It was good to hear the joy of laughter once again. Running out of the room and down the hall the child shouted, "Bet you can't find me again."

Caroline sat down at the table and sighed. "This could go on all day if a body let it! I don't see how Sarah takes it."

"Maybe you're getting in some practice for when you have children," Rosemary smiled.

"Oh, I don't know about that. Thomas and I haven't talked about children," Caroline said.

"Thomas?" Rosemary questioned.

"Yep. Major Thomas Watkins. You know, Henry's brother."

Rosemary's heart lifted. "You mean you are actually going to get that rascal to settle down?" she asked.

"Looks that way. We agreed not to marry until after the war is over, and I do wish it was tomorrow," Caroline said. "So, tell me, cousin. How about your love life? Who's the lucky man you've been seeing?"

Rosemary smiled. "You know I don't have time for a man with all my studies. So, you are finally going to corral that scalawag! I am so happy for you. I have a feeling that most folks think we are fighting for the same man." The two cousins laughed at the thought.

Mama Bonner ended conversation by asking Arkie if he was finished eating. Arkie walked outside. He knew Rosemary's feeling about being alone. Now it was his turn to cheer her up. He walked to the fence so that he could see Molly as he thought on the subject.

Arkie was growing up in a hurry. Experiencing combat and all it's death and almost starving to death had made him realize the value of home and its responsibilities.

But women and their love life would be a new experience for the young man.

He watched as Bonner went to the barn. He wondered if Bonner remembered that Arkie had cut the ropes from his hands just a few days before. Bonner saw him standing by the fence but paid no attention.

It seemed an hour had passed as Arkie stood watching his mare graze. When Bonner finished his chores in the barn, he walked to where Arkie stood. Mama Bonner had told her husband about the conversation between the two women. He admired Rosemary and loved Caroline as his own. "Mr. Carter sho' raises some fine horses, don't he?" Bonner asked.

"That mare is mine!" Arkie replied.

"Sho' nuff? It looks like Mr. Carter's hoss; the one he called Rags," Bonner said.

"Well, it ain't no more! Her name is Molly! He done went and gave her to me," Arkie answered.

Bonner smiled. "Dat was good of Mr. John, and he couldn't have gave it to no one no finer. I wants to thank you again for what you done up there in them hills. Dem folks was about to kill me 'fo you and master John showed up."

"You'd done the same for me, and besides I got to take one of those hot baths my Mama used to tell me about. Did you know John Carter has a big scar down his back?" Arkie asked.

"Yassuh. Everyone knows about that. Caused by a Yankee saber. But Mr. John fixed him. He won't put no more scars on backs," Bonner replied.

"You mean John Carter was in the cavalry?" Arkie asked.

"Him and his two sons. Rode with the Major when the Major was just a Captain," Bonner answered.

"How come he quit?" Arkie asked.

"The Major wouldn't let him fight no more, but his two boys still rode with him 'till last month. He buried one of his sons up there next to his Maw. You and Miss Rosemary fixing to leave in the morning?" Bonner asked.

"We will, unless she changes her mind," Arkie said.

Bonner left Arkie standing at the fence watching his mare graze. This was the first time he had ever owned anything, and the feeling was just great. He tried calling Molly a few times, but she paid no attention. When he whistled she perked up her head as though she was used to that. He tried practicing several whistle calls, but she lowered her head and went back to grazing.

Walking slowly up to her as he had done several times before, he grabbed her mane and mounted her, bareback. Guiding her with his knees, she walked to the gate. Arkie rode her around to the front of the Glass home. His pride was showing in his face, giving it a reddish glow.

"Bring her over here, Arkie, and let me ride," Sarah's oldest said.

"You'd better go ask your Maw about that," he answered.

A few minutes later, the boy came running out the house yelling, "She said I could!"

Still holding her mane, Arkie walked Molly to the edge of the porch so the boy could slide on. He walked the horse around the yard. The boy felt like he was riding into battle as some gallant horseman. Arkie had started something that he might not stop for awhile.

Sarah walked out of the house to check on the situation. "I'm afraid you started something, Arkie. He'll wear you down," Sarah said, laughing.

"Oh, I don't mind, and Molly shore don't. She likes little kids," he answered.

"Well, that's enough. Help him down. He needs to be in here helping me take care of his little sister, anyway," Sarah said, and then to her son, "Tell Arkie thank you."

"Thank you, Arkie, and you too, Molly," he said as he scampered back inside the house.

Still holding on to the horse's mane, Arkie rode Molly back to the pasture and turned her loose, again. From a big open window Rosemary had watched most of what happened. She knew Arkie was a good boy and good with children. Mildred and her girls had grown very fond of him. Gladys looked on him as a big brother.

As evening approached, the entire household sat on the big porch, listening to the quiet country sounds before bedtime. At a distance, near the forest, a whippoorwill sounded its night call.

Sarah sat with all three of her children nearby while Caroline braided her hair. A full moon and a gentle breeze made it a pleasant night. When the whippoorwills would cry out, Sarah's oldest asked, "What are those birds saying when they do that?"

Arkie said, "Why, you don't know? I bet you don't know how they got the name Whippoorwill either, now do you?" The little boy shook his head.

"Well, want me to tell you?" Arkie asked.

Rosemary said, "Tell us Arkie! We're all dying to hear."

"Well, back home, they tell the tale about one of the meanest and toughest black crows in those parts, named Will. He went around, eating up everybody's corn. After he ate up the corn, he went around robbing other birds of everything they had. This was a mean old crow.

"So one day the people got tired of Will and all his dirty deeds, so they went to the preacher and asked him what they could do about it. The preacher had a big green bird called a Polly Parrot that come from somewhere far off in the jungle. They say this Polly Parrot could talk.

"So one night, just after dark, the preacher brought the parrot to this feller's farm so he could catch the black crow eating up the farmer's corn the next morning."

Greater Love Hath No Man

Arkie paused in his story and looked around. All the children had fallen asleep. Caroline picked one of them up and carried the child to bed with Rosemary following with the another, leaving Sarah still sitting in the chair holding her baby.

Turning and looking back before entering the house, Rosemary said, "Arkie, you'll have to finish your story some other time. It's late, and it's been a long day."

When Rosemary went inside, Sarah said, "Go ahead Arkie, and finish your story, if you like."

"Maybe some other time. I think Miss Rosemary is right; it's getting late, and I'm going to sleep in the barn tonight, so I can practice my whistle call on Molly in the morning," Arkie said.

Chapter twenty-two

A heavy dew had fallen across Carter Town, leaving the grass wet, as though a light rain had come during the night.

The screeching sound of the old barn door roused Arkie from his sleep. "If you gonna eat, you might ought to get a move on," cried Bonner. "Dem women folks is already dressed and sittin' at the table."

Arkie walked to the pump and stuck his head under the stream of cold water. Trying to dry his hair quickly, he shook his head until he was almost dizzy.

Bonner asked, "Is you and Miss Rosemary leaving this morning? If you is, after you finish eating your breakfast, if you bring the horses up, I'll hitch them up fo' you."

Bonner rubbed his hand down the side of the coach door. "You know, I don't think I ever sees a big coach like this before."

"Miss Rosemary said her father won it in a poker game in Richmond, before the war," Arkie responded.

"How does it feel, sitting way up there driving all dem horses?" Bonner asked.

"Fine. Just fine. Look inside. This thing has everything. There's even a little door in the top, so whenever Miss Rosemary wants me to know something, she can speak to me from down there. Ain't that all right?" Arkie said.

Bonner stuck his head inside and looked around, saying, "My, my, you sho' nuf can."

Arkie walked to the house, leaving Bonner to look at the coach. Everyone inside was eating. Caroline held the baby, trying to feed it. Dr. Glass had been gone since daylight. Rosemary watched as Arkie removed his hat and sat down.

"After we've finished our breakfast, Arkie, I think it would be best if we should be traveling toward home," she said. Arkie nodded his head, as he began eating.

Bonner was continually walking in and out of the kitchen, carrying something from the barn. "What's he doing?" Rosemary asked

"Oh, he's getting stuff out of that old sutler's wagon Thomas brought here a couple of months back," Caroline said.

The lack of information about Henry was making it more difficult for Rosemary to leave.

Dogs barking in the distance told the Glass family they were about to have company.

"Someone riding in from the west, off old Butcher's tavern trail," Bonner said.

"Well, look and see who it is," Mama Bonner scolded.

Bonner walked out of the house and saw a lone horseman riding up. Hurrying back inside he shouted, "Miss Caroline, it looks like Mr. Carter's friend. That Mr. Dan Holland." Rosemary became fidgety.

"Well, Bonner, go and invite him in," Caroline said.

Rosemary went to her room and began packing.

Arkie had had all of Dan Holland he wanted. He walked out the back door and went to the pasture to try to locate his horse. All the animals were grazing over a small knoll, making it hard for Arkie to see them. If he could catch Molly and saddle her, he could run the coach horses to the barn, and the rest would be easy. Bonner had promised to do all the hitching.

Crossing the fence and trying to whistle for Molly made things worse. The more he whistled, the farther the horses walked away. Molly paid no attention. Giving up the idea as a bad deal, Arkie walked back to the corral to saddle up Bonner's old mule. "Bet I do catch you," he mumbled.

Bonner stood on the porch and greeted the visitor. "Get down Mr. Holland," Bonner said. "Miss Caroline and the others are in the kitchen. Go on inside while I take your horse around to the barn."

Dan dismounted and went inside. He then strolled down the hall. He had been inside the Glass home only once, so he wasn't sure just where the kitchen was.

Rosemary came walking out of her room, almost bumping in to him. "Wh-why, Mr. Holland! What a n-nice surprise," she stammered.

Dan was caught off guard. He couldn't say a word but just stared. Trying to regain his composure he said, "Bonner invited me in, and I'm afraid I've gotten myself lost trying to find the kitchen."

"Well, come on, and I'll escort you to it," Rosemary answered.

Arkie was more than glad to see Bonner walking Dan's mount to the barn. Now he could round up all the horses and herd them into the corral.

"I'll take him," Arkie said.

Bonner handed him the reigns. Arkie went riding off across the pasture like a flash. Bonner stood watching, scratching his woolly head and saying, "That boy chile gonna get himself killed, if he don't watch it."

Meanwhile, Caroline helped Sarah and her children to their room, leaving Rosemary and Dan to get better acquainted, much to the delight of Caroline. Her thoughts ran wild with excitement. She whispered to Sarah, "Ain't love grand?"

Sarah replied, "Only if you got the right beau."

Caroline had forgotten about Sarah's hurt for a moment. "Forgive me Sarah. I wasn't thinking," she begged.

Bonner was startled when something else got his attention. "Miss Caroline!" he called. "There's another rider headed this way, but this time he's a-comin' from the east. Looks like a solider, but I can't make it out just yet."

Caroline ran down the hall and out the front door shouting, "Go fetch Poppa's spyglass, and hurry." Bonner trotted down the hall to the study. The rider had turned off and rode toward John Carter's home before Bonner made it back. He handed the long spyglass to Caroline. "He's done turned off and rode into the timbers. Looks like he might be heading toward John Carter's place. Go hitch up the buggy, and hurry!" she ordered.

"But Miss Caroline, yo' poppa done left in the buggy early this morning to the Ross' house. Mrs. Ross is gonna have a baby," Bonner answered.

"Oh, that's right. Well, go saddle a horse. I've got to find out who that is," she cried.

Trying not to argue, Bonner said quietly, "Miss Caroline, that's not the Major; if'n it was, he'd done been here, and you knows it."

"Perhaps you're right, Bonner. But I just have to know who it is. He looked like one of ours, you say?"

"Miss Caroline, old Bonner couldn't say. He was too far away, and you knows that if it's something all that important, Massuh John gonna let you know."

"I take it you don't want to saddle a horse," she said.

"No ma'am. I'll go saddle your horse, right now. But I think you ought to wait," he said. Bonner walked through the kitchen where Dan and Rosemary were drinking coffee and talking.

"Miss Rosemary, I wish you could talk some sense into Miss Caroline. She's acting funny and wanting me to go saddle her hoss to ride off to see who that rider was."

"What rider?" Rosemary asked.

When Bonner explained what had just happened, Dan said, "I'll go see who it is. You go tell Caroline that I'll be right back." Dan excused himself and walked out the back door.

Bonner watched Dan walk to the barn. "You know, that Massuh Dan is a nice man," he said.

"Yes. I think so too, Bonner," said Rosemary.

Bonner said, "I think we gonna see just how nice he really is when he finds out that mister Arkie done got his hoss and gone to fetch all the rest of dem hosses."

Meanwhile, Chadwick Carter rode up to his father's house and sat patiently waiting for John to come to the door. "Anybody home? Maw! Paw!" Chadwick called out.

John was in the barn pitching hay. He thought he heard a voice but couldn't distinguish where it was coming from. When he came out of the barn he could see just the

Greater Love Hath No Man

rear end of a horse sticking out around the side of the house. John eased up behind him.

Seeing who it was, he said, "Get down. A man's behind gets saddle sores if he sits to long."

Chadwick dismounted and embraced his father. "Where's Maw?" he asked.

"She's gone, son. We buried her a few days ago," John replied.

Chadwick remained silent. The two walked inside the house.

"Was she sick for long?" Chadwick asked.

"No son, Maw was just plain wore out. I think she wanted to go on to be with your grandfather."

Chadwick nodded his head, understanding. "You put her next to Poppa?" He asked.

"Right beside him," John responded. Changing the subject John asked, "What brings you here, and where is the rest of the bunch? Is the Major well?"

"I'll tell you over a hot cup of coffee," Chadwick suggested. The two had a lot to talk about. The first thing that Chadwick said was "You know, you're a state again."

"When did all this come about?" Asked John.

"Day before yesterday, on the twentieth of the month. Yep, it's official. West Virginia is now a state of it's own," he answered

"Is Wheeling gonna be the capitol?" John asked.

"I'm not sure, but probably," Chadwick said. "Paw, the Major sent me to tell you that, but also to warn you that the Yankee Major we left over in the Scot-Irish settlement lived and has sworn revenge. Said he would burn Carter Town again and hang all the survivors."

John stared out the window while Chadwick was talking. "Paw, are you listening?" he asked.

John answered, "I hear you real well, son. Tell me, where is that Yankee Major now, and where are our boys?"

"Major Watkins and our boys are a two day ride from here. We got a whipping at Brandy Station. Hadn't been for Fritz and his boys, General Stuart wouldn't have made it."

"Was you in on that fight?" John asked.

"No sir, we were late for that, but Major Thomas had us down in the Shenandoah Valley, chasing Yankees out."

"How did you learn about West Virginia and Simmons?" John asked.

"It's all in the papers about West Virginia, and we captured a Yankee officer that told the Major about Simmons. Paw, that's not all he told the Major, either. You ain't going to like what I'm fixing to tell you next. They got Major Watkins' brother with them, too."

"Henry!" cried John.

"Swore to hang him, along with all the survivors of Carter Town. Said he would make examples out of those that still waved the Rebel flag," Chadwick replied. The conversation stopped when they heard hoof beats. Looking out the window Chadwick said, "Rider coming from the Glass' home."

John walked out onto the porch and smiled, as Dan Holland asked permission to get down. "Mineral Wells didn't want you either, I see," John said, laughing.

"Ain't nothing in Mineral Wells pretty as what you got around here," Dan answered.

"Well, you're at the wrong place for all that. She's up at the good doctor's house. Get down Dan, and come inside," John said.

Dan was surprised when Chadwick met him at the door. Hugging Chadwick, Dan said, "Well, look what the buzzards dropped down out of the sky! How you been Chad?" Dan asked.

"Come on, fellows," John interrupted. "I still got some hot coffee back here on the stove. What y'all say we finish it off. Dan, I'm glad you've come. There's some things that Chad has told me I think you should know."

Chapter twenty-three

The fact that Simmons was alive didn't surprise Dan, but the part about Henry being his prisoner did. He searched John's face as Chadwick finished his report. The room became silent.

At the same moment John and Dan said, "Bait."

"Won't work. The Major knew it, right off," Chadwick replied.

John and Dan both knew better than to ask what the Major's plans were. Chadwick walked outside to relieve himself, leaving John and Dan talking. As he started back into the house, he noticed a surrey traveling down the main road toward the Glass home. "Looks like Carter Town is getting a visitor," Chadwick mused, as he walked back into the room.

John walked outside and stood on the front porch. "Now I wonder who could that be," he said. Dan joined him on the porch.

"They're kicking up too much dust for me to make out," Dan said.

Standing in the doorway, Chadwick replied, "Well, who ever it is, they sure have got a pretty rig."

"Maybe a body should go and find out," smiled Dan.

"And you're that somebody," John said with a laugh.

"Well, somebody needs to find out. Looks like they're heading for the Glass house," Dan said, walking to his horse. Mounting, he looked back at John and winked.

Chadwick asked as Dan rode out of sight, "What was that all about?"

"It's called love sick, my boy. Something you wouldn't know nothing about, right now, but someday you might," John answered.

"You mean Dan has got a hankering for Caroline?" Chadwick asked.

"Not Caroline, son. Miss Rosemary," John said.

"I'm missing out on something here. Who's Miss Rosemary?"

"It's a long story. Let's finish that coffee while I explain," John answered.

Meanwhile Dan rode to a place where he could see Bonner helping a lady and two small girls down from the surrey. An elderly, well-dressed man stood brushing at his clothes trying to remove the dust. Dan watched as Bonner escorted them to the front porch of the Glass home. Rosemary came running out of the house and embraced them. Mystified and not wanting to intrude, he rode back to John's place.

"Was it Jeff Davis and his family?" John asked.

"You know, I'm really not sure, but whoever they are, Rosemary knew them, because she hugged all four of them," Dan answered.

"Was it a woman and two little girls?" John asked.

"Yes, and a well-dressed old man, too," Dan answered.

"I'm not sure about the old man, but I bet a ten-dollar gold piece that's Henry's wife, Mildred and his girls," John said thoughtfully.

"I hope that's Henry's family, in a way, but in another I hope it ain't. Fellows, I think I'll take a ride to the good doctor's home and find out for myself. Mind if I borrow your horse, Dan?" John asked.

"Go right ahead. He probably knows the way better than you," Dan laughed.

Winking at Chadwick on his way out, John replied, "Yep, I bet he does."

Chadwick left Dan sitting at the table as he went outside and drew a bucket of water from the well.

"You gonna take a bath?" Dan asked.

"I aim to try and clean myself up some, and if I can find some clean clothes around here, I'm gonna change," Chadwick answered.

"You know, if I had a change I'd probably join you," Dan said.

"There ought to be some of Eli's clothes here. I believe they might fit you," Chadwick suggested.

"Too bad about Eli," Dan said sadly. Chadwick remained silent.

When John returned, he found the two sitting on the front porch, clean and with a change of clothes. "Well, what brought all this on? Ain't no fun-loving event that I know of going on around here," John said.

"What did you find out?" Chadwick asked.

John answered, "Bittersweet."

With his brow wrinkled in bewilderment, Dan looked at Chadwick. "Now, what do you suppose he meant by that?"

"Knowing my Paw, who could guess?" Chadwick responded.

Arkie came riding up on the bay horse that John had given him. Seeing the two men on the porch, he dismounted and walked to where they sat. "Isn't that Rags that fellow just rode up on?" asked Chadwick quietly.

"Yeah. I'll let your Paw tell you all about that," Dan whispered.

Seeing Arkie, John quickly introduced him to Chadwick. "I saw you when you rode away from the doctor's place. What's going on?" asked Arkie.

"I was just about to ask you the same question," John smiled. "Is that Henry's family?" he asked.

"Yeah, and brought Miss Rosemary's father, too," Arkie replied.

With a slight touch of arrogance he covered with a smile, Dan said, "Looks like Carter Town got two brother doctors on hand. One a Yankee and the other a Reb. Things are going to get very interesting around here."

John poured a cup of coffee for Arkie. "Sit down, and chew the fat with us. We've just been discussing all the current events. Maybe you could shed some light on the subject of just what's going on at the good doctor's house," John said, his curiosity unabashed.

"Ain't much to tell, other than Mrs. Watkins and Rosemary seemed to be spending a lot of time talking. The girls are playing with Miss Sarah's children," Arkie responded.

"Well, how about the two doctors? Are they going at it?" Dan asked.

"Heck no! They were so glad to see each other that they both cried like babies," Arkie said.

John sipped his coffee. "Like I was saying, bittersweet."

Chadwick spit out his coffee. "Paw, we drank better coffee than this in the field. What is this stuff, anyway? Chicken droppings?" he asked.

"Parched okra and some other stuff. Coffee has beer scarce around here. The only time I get a real cup of coffee is when I visit the doctor's house," John said, laughing.

"That old sutler wagon they got in the barn has plenty," Arkie said.

"That must be the wagon the Major was telling us about," Chadwick said.

"Fellows, I need to get back. I just wanted to see what you might have on your mind, Mister John," Arkie said.

"Don't leave until I write you out a bill of sale," John said.

"Why you giving him Rags, Paw?" Chadwick asked.

"Because I want to," John answered.

"Paw, you know Eli broke Rags and even named her. Why you doing this?" Chadwick asked again.

John finished writing out the bill of sale and handed it to Arkie. "That should do it."

Arkie stared at the paper for a few minutes and then handed it back to John. "No, sir. I can't do this. I don't want her. She needs to stay here with you and Chadwick. Besides, when we leave here, I'm sure I'll be busy driving that big coach of Miss Rosemary's," Arkie said sadly.

John looked at Chadwick with a firm stare. "You stay out of this! Arkie, I gave Molly, the saddle, and the

Greater Love Hath No Man

bridle to you, and besides, you can tie her off to the back of the coach. She'll follow just fine. Now that's the way it is! Understood?"

Reluctantly, Arkie folded the paper and placed it in his shirt pocket.

Chadwick walked to the barn without saying a word, leaving Dan looking out the window. "Think I'll mosey on up to the good doctor's house and see what's going on up there. Care to ride together, Arkie?" Dan asked. Arkie understood it was time to go.

"John, I'll see about getting you some real coffee while I'm there," said Dan. The two left the room, leaving John looking toward the barn.

After Dan and Arkie rode away, John walked to the barn where Chadwick was brushing his horse. He knew not to rekindle the spark of the previous conversation. When he walked in, Chadwick ignored him.

As John approached the rear of Chadwick's horse, he said, "Ever notice how those little mud balls form underneath a horse's mane when you ride in a lot of dust?"

"You telling me I need to cut my mare's mane?" Chadwick asked angrily.

"No, son. I was just trying to make conversation."

"Well, for your information, I'm going to cut her mane before I leave here. Anything else wrong?" Chadwick asked.

John knew anything else he said would only make things worse. He slowly walked back to the house.

When Dan and Arkie rode up to the Glass' barn, Bonner came walking up. Dan walked to the sutler's wagon and began rummaging through it, searching for coffee. "Massuh Dan, what is you looking fo'? Maybe I can help you find it," Bonner said.

"I'm looking for some coffee for John Carter. I'm tired of drinking that poison he calls coffee," Dan answered.

"Miss Caroline had me to bring all the coffee to the house. You knows she'll send Mr. John some, if you ask," Bonner said.

Dan climbed down from the wagon.

"Stinks! Smells like something died in there," he said.

"I don't smell nothing. That's where I catches up on some naps sometimes," Bonner answered.

Arkie walked out the back door, eating a piece of fried chicken. Wiping his hands on the leg of his trousers, he said, "Hey Dan, Mama Bonner got some fried chicken in there. Sure is good."

"You see Miss Rosemary in there?" Dan asked.

"She's in the kitchen, giving Sarah's baby a bath," Arkie said.

Dan walked to the back door. "Think I'll take you up on that chicken."

When Rosemary saw Dan walk in she became nervous. Trying to dry the child, she almost dropped her. Dan and Rosemary grabbed the child at the same time, bringing them face-to-face.

Without hesitation, Dan kissed her. In a willing moment, she kissed him back. They gazed into each other's eyes. Stuttering, Dan began trying to make excuses. At that moment, Caroline came walking in to the room.

"Ahem," she said. "Pardon me. Let me take the baby, while you two go on about your business." Caroline took the child and left the room. Dan and Rosemary spent much time embracing and kissing one another. Arkie, trying to pretend he hadn't noticed, interrupted the two.

"Did you get any of that chicken, yet, Dan?" He asked. Rosemary left the room and walked down the hall.

"Yeah. I mean no, not yet. I seemed to have gotten delayed for a minute," Dan said.

"Huh! More liked stopped dead in your tracks, if you asked me," Arkie said.

"No one asked you! Now, where is that chicken?"

Chapter twenty-four

While the Glass family was enjoying their company from Mineral Wells, General Lee was pushing his Confederate army toward the small town of Gettysburg, Pennsylvania.

Major Watkins' ragtag bunch had disbursed their spoils of war and had gone back to their homes, leaving only the Major and four men.

Simmons and his command, along with several militiamen were camped near Deer Run. Henry Watkins sat on a log with his hands freed from his bonds and was eating, when a whisper came from a bush behind him.

"Mr. Watkins, I'll get you out of this somehow."

Henry never twitched a muscle, but sat quietly eating.

The union guard squatted in front of him and asked, "You about finished, fellow?"

"Just about," Henry answered.

"When you do, the Major wants to see you," the guard growled.

Henry's mind was starting to play tricks on him. *Did I hear a voice from behind me, or was I imagining things again?* he wondered.

For days, he had imagined his bother riding out of the thick timbers, coming to his rescue. At night, in his dreams, he saw Thomas waiting around every bend of the trail. Several times he dreamed the same thing about two men holding a flag, shouting, "Mountaineers are always free!" It was so real, he longed to share it, but he was a prisoner. No one cared to here what he had to say.

"Let's go!" The guard commanded. Standing and stretching his long legs, Henry stuck his hands out for the guard to secure him again.

"Major said to leave them off for now." Nudging Henry toward the command tent, the guard walked behind him.

Henry went inside and found Simmons sitting at a small table, drinking coffee. "You get enough to eat?" Simmons asked. Henry didn't answer.

"You look like something that lives in a cave," Simmons said cruelly. Henry still refused to say anything. "Sergeant!" Simmons shouted. Simmons was furious as he ordered that Henry be clean shaven and for his hair to be cut.

"I'm gonna hang you and that Rebel brother of yours, as well as all those cutthroats he calls soldiers he has with him!" He screamed.

On the way out, Henry mumbled, "We'll see about that." As he walked back to the log he had previously sat on, he thought he recognized a young private walking in front of him. *Could that be the Baker boy?*

Trying not to be conspicuous he turned his head and sat down. If that was the Baker boy, then maybe it wasn't my imagination after all, he thought.

The sergeant tied Henry's hands together once more. "You must have done something besides being a spy to get the Major riled up like that," he said.

"I ain't no spy. Is that what he's been telling you fellows?" Henry asked.

"Don't matter none. You're still my prisoner, and that's the way it is," he answered.

Henry knew it was hopeless to try to discuss the matter any further. "That private that walked by us, when we came out, what's his name?" Henry asked.

"Fellow, I'm ordered to see you get a shave and a haircut before the Major hangs you, not to answer questions," the sergeant responded.

Henry sat with his hands bound together, waiting for someone to come and follow Simmons' orders. The mosquitoes were terrible. He moved down to the end of the log, hoping the smoke from the soldier's fire might give him some relief. His hair was long and tangled. Simmons was right about one thing. His appearance did make him look like some cave man.

While Henry sat patiently waiting for the unit's barber, his brother Thomas and three others were en route to Carter Town. Knowing that he would be no match in a fight, Thomas chose to cross several miles north of Simmons' camp at a place called Cub Run. This would put him much closer to Carter Town.

Meanwhile, at the Glass' house, plans were being made for a social. There would be a dance in the barn with hill folks coming from miles around. Miners and their families would also be there. The celebration of statehood was the main reason.

Rosemary and Caroline had made a flag that would be displayed on a pole in front of the barn. Mountaineers would be bringing their finest jugs of corn liquor along with the best of barbeque. It would be the biggest celebration that Carter Town had ever known.

John Carter's and Arkie's job was to ride to the mountains and pass the word. Dan Holland and Chadwick rode up to mine country to invite everyone there. Afterwards they all were to meet at the hot springs for a bath. The sun had started setting behind high peaks as Dan and Chadwick stopped at the springs. They were the first there.

"You know, you'd think Paw and Arkie would have been here before us," Chadwick said.

Dan pulled off his clothes and waded into the warm water. "They'll be along directly. Come on in. The water's fine. There's some soap in my saddlebag. Throw it to me, if you don't mind," Dan asked politely. Chadwick tossed him the soap. "You coming in?" Dan asked.

"I'm going to wait on Paw and Arkie. They should have been here," Chadwick said worriedly.

"Oh, come on in. They'll be along directly."

Chadwick must have believed him. In less than a minute he had stripped and was splashing around like a duck.

They were acting like small schoolboys, splashing water on each other when John and Arkie rode up. "I could hear you over on the other side of the mountain," John called to them.

Arkie leaped from his horse like a frog. "Last one in is a rotten egg!" Arkie shouted at John.

When the four were through with their baths Chadwick asked, "Paw, what took you so long?"

"He had a little meeting with a bunch of mountaineers," Arkie said with a grin.

"If we gonna get home before dark, we might ought to think about riding," John said. The four horsemen walked their mounts single file down the slope toward Carter Town.

At the end of the trail, Arkie and Dan went toward the Glass' house. "See y'all," said Dan.

"Oh Rosemary, my sweet, sweet Rosemary," teased Chadwick, as he looked at Dan.

Dan snickered, then replied, "Well, your day will come, and when it does, old John won't be able to hold you back. Ain't that right John?"

Throwing up his hand in a wave, John answered, "See you fellows." He and Chadwick rode toward home.

It was dark by the time Dan and Arkie stopped in front of the Glass' barn. Bonner was nowhere in sight. "You going inside after you put up your horse?" Arkie asked.

"Sure; got my bath, and I feel and smell better. Ain't you?" Dan asked.

"Think I'll bed down early," Arkie answered.

"Suit yourself. I'm going inside to get some vittles, if there are any," Dan said. He lit two lanterns, taking one with him and leaving the other for Arkie. "If they got something to eat in there, want me to send some out by Bonner?" Dan asked.

Trying to close the barn door, Arkie answered, "If you want to."

Dan walked into the kitchen and found the two Glass brothers at the table, talking. "Hope I'm not interrupting anything." he said.

"Not at all. Come in, Mr. Holland. I want you to meet my brother from Mineral Wells, another doctor Glass." Dan shook the visitor's hand.

"So, you're the young man that my daughter has been telling me about," he said.

"Uh, y-yes sir. I-I mean I think so," Dan stuttered.

The visiting doctor tried to push away thoughts about Dan serving the Confederacy. "How long have you been in the Confederate army?" he asked.

Dan thought a moment about the question. "I'm not in the army, but I do fight aggression when the opportunity arises, just as any good Yankee would do if I went to their homes and burned them out," Dan answered.

Rosemary's father cleared his throat. "Yes. I suppose you would." The night was slowly slipping away as the three men talked.

Dan excused himself with a yawn. "Gentlemen, it's been a pleasure, but I'm going to the barn to turn in," he said sleepily. He had forgotten all about eating and getting something for Arkie to eat. He left the two brothers talking, took his lantern and walked to the barn.

The next morning Bonner woke Arkie while humming a tune as he cleaned out the stalls. "Don't you know any other tune besides a race track five miles long?" Arkie asked.

"Sho do, Massuh Arkie, I knows 'do da, do da.'" he laughed as Arkie threw one of his boots at him playfully. "Why, Massuh Arkie, don't you want old Bonner to sing to you this here fine morning?"

Dan was lying on a hay pile in the corner, snoring. "I don't know which is worse, putting up with old Dan over there making all that noise or your do da song," Arkie said, laughing.

Bonner, smiling happily, handed Arkie his boot. "Sorry, Massuh Arkie. Mama Bonner has some good-smelling biscuits and red eye gravy in the house." Arkie staggered to the pump, and as always, stuck his head under the stream of water, trying to wake himself.

It was a beautiful morning. Sunlight was coming through tops of tall timbers, and a light fog resembled smoke from slow burning campfires. In the distance, Bob White quails sounded their call.

Arkie raked his hands through his hair, put on his cap, and walked in the house. He could see the Glass family at the table, as he stood in the kitchen door way.

"Sit yourself down, Master Arkie, and Mama Bonner will get you some of those hot biscuits and gravy. You musta smelled dem all the way out to da barn," Mama Bonner smiled.

Removing his cap, Arkie sat down as Mama Bonner prepared his plate.

"Did you and Mr. Holland sleep well?" Rosemary asked. Arkie nodded politely. "Where is Mr. Holland? Is he coming to breakfast?" She asked.

"He's still asleep, ma'am," he answered.

Rosemary finished her breakfast and asked Mama Bonner to fix Dan a cup of coffee.

"You want that I take it to him?" Mama Bonner asked.

"No, I'll take it to him," she replied. Rosemary walked to the barn. Seeing Bonner, she said, "I think Mama Bonner needs you in the house."

Rosemary put the coffee down and began tickling Dan under the nose with a straw. He would try to blow it away, and when he got wise to her prank, he pretended he was asleep. When she looked away, he pulled her to him. They laughed and kicked like school kids.

She said, "We're gonna knock this coffee over, if you don't be careful."

"You care? I don't," Dan said.

Getting up, she said, "You might when it spills on your leg."

He pulled her back down. "I don't care. I got a doctor that can patch things up for me."

Greater Love Hath No Man

The two were kissing when Arkie came walking in. Clearing his throat, Arkie said, "Miss Rosemary, your father was asking about you awhile ago."

Rosemary got up and brushed at her dress. "Arkie, not a word of this, you hear!" she ordered.

"Yes, ma'am!" He answered.

Dan sat up and took a drink of his coffee. "You know you could have stayed at John Carter's last night."

"Did I mess things up for you?" Arkie asked, grinning.

When Rosemary went inside the house, Bonner came walking back to the barn. "You gonna be riding this morning?" Bonner asked Arkie.

"Yeah. Going over to John Carter's sometime today, unless Miss Rosemary is ready to go," Arkie replied.

"Well, the smithy brought those new shoes for your mare by here yesterday. Want me to put them on her this morning?" Bonner asked.

Dan walked by the two. "That ain't no hard answer. Why Bonner, you know he does," he said.

"Don't pay no attention to him. It's pay-back time. I'll shoe her myself. But, thanks anyway."

"Yassuh," Bonner replied, as he went back to cleaning the stalls.

It was almost noon when Arkie finished shoeing his horse.

Sarah's oldest child had been playing near the timbers when he came running to Arkie. "There's a man over there behind those trees; I saw him," the boy said.

Arkie lead his mare to the corral. Glancing at the timberline, he noticed a Federal solider crouched behind a fallen log. He sent the boy to the house. "Go tell Mr. Dan, but don't tell him so everyone can hear. Just walk up and whisper in his ear what you saw and then stay inside with your mother. Will you do that for me?" Arkie asked.

The little boy ran to the house and did as Arkie told him.

A few minutes later, Dan came walking out, buckling his pistol belt around his waist. He saw Arkie standing by the corral fence.

Walking as though nothing was happening, Dan whispered, "Where?"

Acting like they were looking at Molly and pointing, Arkie whispered. "In the trees to your left; near the road."

"Can you get a shot at him from where you are?" Dan whispered.

"He's too far away," Arkie said.

"I'll get my rifle," Dan said.

"No need. He's gone now," Arkie sighed.

Greater Love Hath No Man

Chapter twenty-five

Upon hearing about the solider incident, John Carter saddled his mount and rode south, toward the Scot-Irish settlement, leaving Chadwick at home. He knew if he were caught, his chances of talking his way out of trouble would be much greater than Chadwick's. Over the years John had built a good rapport with the Scot-Irish people. It was they who had given him the black corn that Dan took to Henry. If Simmons were in the vicinity, they would know.

Things were quiet when John stopped his mount in front of their church. Not even a bird in the sky. John felt as though someone was watching every move he made.

The pastor's living quarters were behind the church. He dismounted and knocked on the church door. He knocked several times, but no one came. As he walked to the rear of the building, he noticed several fresh hoof prints. It was Thursday, so he knew they were too new to belong to the congregation.

Walking back to his horse, he noticed something lying in the grass. He pushed the tall grass aside with his foot to see what it was. There was a canteen with the initials U.S. stamped in the center. No doubt the Federals had been there. But was it Simmons?

John mounted and slowly walked his horse toward the settlement. The road had a bend, making it difficult to see directly into the village, but he could hear the sound of a wagon rumbling toward him. Guiding his mount to the side of the road, he waited patiently for the wagon to round the turn.

It was a young boy. "Pull up there!" shouted John. The lad stopped his team. "By chance, would you know the whereabouts of the pastor of that church on the hill?" John asked.

"Yes, sir. Pastor Goodnight is in the village with the troops."

"You wouldn't, by chance, know who'd be in charge of our troops, would you?" John asked.

"Oh, yes sir. My Paw said he's a tough one. The Rebels tried to kill him once, but he was too tough to die," the lad responded.

"This tough officer, would you happen to know his name?" John asked.

"Paw said his name was Simmons. They got a spy with them. Gonna hang him, my Maw said."

John had his answer. Thanking the boy, he turned his mount and rode back to Carter Town. Simmons was just four miles away. When John rode to his home, Chadwick wasn't there. Knowing the information he had would start a panic among the women, he decided to remain silent until he could get Dan and the others off to one side and then explain.

Chadwick and Arkie were moving things out of the Glass' barn when he rode up. Dan was supervising the whole affair, until Rosemary came walking up. Reaching for Dan's hand Rosemary asked, "You straw bossing while the others work?"

"Just taking a break," Dan said.

Chadwick winked at Arkie as they sat a wooden feed box down. "Did you hear what he said?" Chadwick asked.

"Yeah. It's his break time," Arkie mumbled.

"Hey, Dan, want to give us a hand for a moment?" Chadwick asked.

Releasing Dan's hand, Rosemary said, "Best I get back inside." As she started back to the house, she passed John Carter sitting on his horse. "You come to oversee the straw boss?" she asked.

John laughed, "Always did make me tired watching other people do all the work." He watched as she walked inside the house.

This would be his opportunity to let the men know what he had found out. Dismounting and tying his horse to the coral fence, he motioned for Dan to come. "Get the others. I've got something to tell you fellows," John said.

Dan walked back inside the barn and motioned for them to come to where he was. "What's going on?" Arkie asked.

"John has something to tell us," he answered.

The three walked to where John stood. "Fellows, we need to keep this quiet as we can from the women folk. Simmons is in the settlement." A hush came over all three.

"What's the plan?" Dan finally broke the silence.

"Not sure, yet. How much you lack being finished here?" John asked.

"We're about finished with the heavy stuff. The women can come in now and start hanging the ribbons and banners, if they want to. Why? Think we might need to go with you or something?" Dan asked.

"No. Go on with your work. I'm going to ride up to the hills. I should be back by dark. Chadwick, if I'm not home by dark, be sure to feed the stock," John ordered. The three watched as John rode out of sight.

Dan walked to the fence post where he had left his pistol belt hanging. Strapping it around his waist, he drew the pistol and checked to see how many rounds he had in it. The others did likewise.

"When the women come out to put up the banners and ribbons, if any ask why we got on our guns, just say it's in case we see a snake or something," Dan suggested.

"Miss Caroline ain't gonna swallow that," Arkie replied.

"Well, use any excuse. Just don't let them suspect anything, you hear?" Dan ordered.

Henry's wife Mildred and their two girls came out, carrying a wide roll of ribbon. "Here, let me help you with that," Arkie offered.

Handing him the long roll, Mildred replied, "Why, thank you, Arkie."

Gladys climbed up to the loft. "Chunk it up here, if you can, Arkie, and I'll tie it around this post," she said.

Arkie tossed it to her. "Good catch," he said. Gladys smiled back. After tying the ribbon, she tossed it to the other side. Violet climbed up and tied the other end around another post. This went on and on until the complete roll was streaming from one side to the other.

"Looks good," Caroline commented, as she walked inside.

"Aunt Caroline, catch me when I jump," Violet said.

"No! You climb down just like you went up, young lady, or your mother will tan both our hides," Caroline answered.

Mildred knew that Caroline would handle it just fine. "This is going to be a big shindig. I wish Poppa could be here," Gladys said.

"You never know, bright eyes. The good lord might just fix it so he will," Mildred responded.

"I been praying for Poppa," Gladys said.

"So have I, sweetheart," she answered.

The town blacksmith drove up in his wagon, and as he got down, he looked around saying, "My, my. You ladies have done a good job in decorating this place. Don't even look like a barn, now."

Dan walked to the smithy's wagon. "You bring the stuff to make the fireworks?" he asked

"Two kegs of it, but we might ought to wait before making any, in case something goes wrong. Don't want to take a chance, having these women and kids around," he said.

Arkie walked around, looking at his wagon. "You got black powder in them kegs?" He asked.

The smithy looked at Dan, astonished.

"You got to overlook him. He's from Arkansas," Dan joked.

The smithy walked to the rear of the wagon. "Let's set these down somewhere out of the way," the smithy ordered. Picking up one of the kegs and placing it on his shoulder, he carried it to the corral gate.

Dan did likewise, while Arkie watched. "Don't just stand there! Get the rest of the stuff out of the wagon," Dan growled at Arkie.

"Yassuh, boss," Arkie answered.

Dan wanted to warn the smithy about Simmons, but he wasn't sure how. "You got any more of this stuff at your place?" Dan asked.

"In that old shed down by the creek. Miners come down sometimes and buy it," he answered.

Rosemary brought the men a tray of several small glasses of lemonade. Arkie was the first to reach for one. "No, thank you," the smithy responded. "I'm gonna head back to the shop. I'm sure Arkie will help you dispose of it."

Dan drank his without stopping. The sourness made him wink his right eye shut. "Whew! That's got a mule's kick to it!" he exclaimed.

Bonner came, dragging a tarp from the old sutler's wagon. "Mr. Dan, think we might ought to cover that stuff up, in case it rains?" He asked.

Dan helped him stretch the canvas, while Arkie and Chadwick walked back into the barn. Dan whispered, "Bonner, I need to talk to you about something."

"Yassuh, Master Dan. I'm listening," Bonner whispered.

"How many guns and ammunition are there around here?" He asked.

"Well, let's see, I got my shotgun and a few shells but they're old and Miss Caroline's got that little double barrel she carries in her little drawstring purse. I don't know how many bullets she has, but she sho' knows how to use it," Bonner said.

"Is that all?" Dan asked.

"Yassuh. What you want to know all that fo', Master Dan?" Bonner asked.

"Don't say anything about this to anyone. You hear me? Especially the women and the children," Dan ordered.

"You can trust old Bonner, Mister Dan," Bonner replied soberly.

"We might have some visitors soon, and I'm sure they won't be friendly. Think you can slip off and get word to the Davenports without being missed?" Dan asked.

"I can send Hezekiah. He'll do all right," Bonner said.

"Well, send him. Just be sure to tell him not a word of this to anyone but old man Davenport. Understood?" Dan ordered.

"Mr. Dan, is dem Yankees coming to burn us out again?" Bonner asked, sadly.

"I don't know yet. Just tell them the shindig will start tomorrow and to come toting." Bonner walked back to the house. Dan could hear Bonner when he called for Hezekiah.

Mama Bonner came out the back door. "What's you want with that boy? He's peeling taters."

"You never mind. I's got something I needs him to do," Bonner answered.

"Hezekiah! Oh, Hezekiah!" She shouted. Hezekiah wasn't peeling potatoes. He was sleeping soundly in the cellar. When Mama Bonner found him, she swatted him across the buttocks with a broom and shouted, "You get out there and see what's yo' Poppa want wif you, right now."

Scratching his rear, he ran all the way to the barn. Bonner saddled the mule and relayed the message. Dan watched as Hezekiah rode toward the mountains.

"Where's he going?" Arkie asked.

"Davenports," whispered Dan.

Greater Love Hath No Man

Chapter twenty-six

A lone horseman dressed as a farmer walked his mount to the command tent in Simmons' camp. Dismounting and handing the bridle reigns to a nearby sentry, he said, "Let the Major know I'm back." He looked at Henry sitting on a log trying to drink coffee with his hands tied. The horseman spit out a cud of tobacco and asked, "That coffee you're drinking, is it any good?" Henry knew who he was. "I asked you a question," he scolded.

Henry slowly sipped at his brew.

"I heard you." The rider sat down on a log, facing Henry.

The sergeant walked up. "The Major will see you now," he reported. The man was still staring at Henry, as he walked with the sergeant to Simmons' tent.

Inside, Simmons acted as though he was glad to see him. "Well, what did you find out?" Simmons asked anxiously.

"They crossed Cub Run just as you suspected and camped about a mile or so from Carter Town," he replied.

Hitting the table with his fist, Simmons screamed, "Perfect! Now I've got the bastard!"

"Something else you might ought to know," continued the man.

"Well, speak up, man!" Simmons shouted.

"He's only got three men with him."

"Hot damn! I have him for sure now," Simmons growled.

Meanwhile, near Davenport Gap, Hezekiah was having difficulties in trying to settle his mule. The need of having to walk a narrow ledge troubled the animal.

"Come on mule," Hezekiah commanded. "you gonna be all right." The old mule refused to go. The rock ledge was mostly loose shale, making it hard to walk on without sliding, and the old mule wasn't taking any chances.

Dismounting and pulling on the reigns, Hezekiah began to cry. "Oh, come on mule. Ain't no sense in you acting this way. We got to find them Davenports for Poppa," he whined. Hezekiah didn't have to worry about finding the Davenports. Two of the old man's boys were behind some large rocks, laughing so hard at times they had difficulty breathing.

When they slowed their laughter, one of them asked the other "Reckon we ought to help that young darkie?" The two walked to Hezekiah.

"Looks like that there mule got more sense than you. He don't want to walk across that loose shale, carrying no nigger, now does he, brother?"

"Yep. That's right, brother. He might fall off the cliff and break a leg, or even worse, might even get himself killed," said the other brother. Hezekiah waited patiently for their little joke to end.

"What you doing up here, anyway, nigger?" one of the brothers asked.

"My poppa sent me to tell old man Davenport something."

"We're Davenports," one of the brothers piped up.

"If I tell you, will you let me go?" Hezekiah cried.

"Boy, aint nobody holding you, so spit it out."

Hezekiah took a deep breath and released it, saying, "Poppa say Yankees gonna burn Carter Town, again; he says come toting."

When the brothers heard this, one of them went to the top of the mountain and blew a cow horn that made a fearful sound. The other brother turned the mule around for Hezekiah and headed him back down the slope.

"Get on, boy, and go tell your poppa we'll be there."

Hezekiah mounted the old mule and rode slowly down the slope.

When old man Davenport heard the news, he sent one of his youngest up to the mines to inform the others that John Carter was in trouble. When he got there, most of them had left for Carter Town for the celebration. When he learned of the event he rode hard back to his father's. When the old man learned of the social, he called a family meeting.

There would be sixty-two Davenports, including the women and children going to a celebration, but this time even the women and some of the children carried guns.

Greater Love Hath No Man

Sixteen wagons made a long train coming down the side of Davenport mountain.

Carter Town was filling up with people from all over the countryside. It would be more than just a Fourth of July celebration for some, and without knowledge to most, West Virginia would be also honored back into statehood.

Caroline stood with her hands on her hips, trying to direct Arkie and Dan, as they held up the flag that she and Sarah had made. "A little more to the right. Not so high up. Lower it a little," she instructed Arkie.

With nails in his mouth and the hammer in his hand, Dan mumbled, "Here. Right here."

"That'll do fine for now," Caroline said as she walked away.

"Just tie the thing," Dan said. When the two came down the ladders Dan stood back and looked at the flag. "Not bad, even if I do say so myself."

"What's it say?" Arkie asked.

"See those two people standing on each side of that rock with June 20, 1863 on it?" Dan asked.

"Yeah, but what does it say in that writing?" Arkie asked.

"It says, 'state of west Virginia,'" Dan replied.

"Is that the President and Vice President on it?" Arkie asked.

"Are all the people that live in Arkansas as dumb as you?" Dan asked. "One is a farmer and the other is a miner. That's what they do for a living in West Virginia."

"Oh. Why did they write on that there tombstone all that writing? Did somebody die?" Arkie asked.

"I'm going in the house to get something to drink and leave you here figuring it out," Dan growled.

Arkie walked to where Chadwick was sitting. "I been watching you two. Got that flag figured out yet?" Chadwick asked.

"No, but it's sure pretty, though," Arkie answered.

Seeing Mildred and the girls carrying something, Chadwick walked to them. "May I carry those things for you, ma'am?" he asked.

She handed him the bundle. "Why, thank you. Just set them down on that long bench, and I'll tend to them later."

Chadwick did as she asked. Violet sat her bundle down next to it and asked, "What's you're name?"

"Chadwick Carter," he answered. "What's yours?"

"Violet Watkins. The Yankees got my poppa and won't let him come home. Do you know my poppa?" She asked.

"No, sweetheart, but my poppa does, and they're good friends," Chadwick said.

"Are you a Rebel solider, like Arkie?" She asked.

"Sometimes," Chadwick responded.

Mildred interrupted their conversation. "Little lady, you're needed back in the house, helping your sister." Then glancing at Chadwick, Mildred said, "She'll talk your ears off if you let her. I hope she wasn't a bother."

Smiling, Chadwick said, "Oh, no ma'am. She was no bother. I enjoyed talking to her. She's quite a little girl."

Hezekiah stopped his mule near the corral gate. Chadwick saw him as he dismounted. Bonner went to Hezekiah and said, "You git done what I told you?"

Pulling the bridle off the mule, Hezekiah answered, "Yassuh. I do like you says."

The barn was ready now, and people were making camp all over the yard. The street was filled with wagons and the big event would start in a few hours. It would be a two-day and two-night affair, with music and dancing. While the women were displaying all sorts of food on different tables, the men would be off in the shadows, busy pulling the cork from the jug.

While things were in their final stage of preparing to start, far of in another state, history was being made. General Lee's army was being defeated at a place called Gettysburg, Pennsylvania.

Rosemary and Dan walked out of the house and strolled toward the barn. "Have you seen your Paw?" Dan asked Chadwick.

"No. He didn't come home last night, and I haven't seen him at all today," Chadwick said.

"Well, there's a bunch of miners here, but your poppa's not with them," Dan replied.

Rosemary left the two men talking and walked inside the barn.

"I can't figure out why he would take that old buffalo rifle with him. They ain't no buffalos around here," Chadwick said.

"He showed it to me one time. That thing will kill a buffalo over five hundred yards away," Dan said.

"If he shows, I'll tell him you're looking for him," Chadwick said. Dan nodded at Chadwick then walked inside the barn, where Rosemary was talking to some of the miners' wives.

Taking Dan's hand, she excused herself and walked outside with him. They strolled around, welcoming different people. The Watkins girls and two of Sarah's were part of over seventy children that were busy playing different games.

When the Davenports reached the vicinity, they camped near John Carter's place. If Yankees came from the west or southwest, they were ready. On the other end of town, near the river, several mountaineer families had made camp. The only way that Simmons could come without being seen would be from behind the Glass home, through thick and dense forest.

Dogs from the mountaineers' camp starting barking at four approaching riders. It was Thomas and his men.

The breeze blowing the plume feathers in his hat made him look debonair, as he rode in front of the mountaineers' wagons. "Major, what're all these people doing here?" one of his men asked.

"Not sure, but we're about to find out," he said. They couldn't cut across the yard like always because of so many people and their camp sites.

Bonner was the first to see them coming. Running as fast as he could, he shouted, "Miss Caroline! Miss Caroline! Da Major! Da Major is coming!" When she heard Bonner, she knew instantly what was happening. Running out the house with her arms open and tears streaming down her face, she ran to greet him.

Without completely stopping his mount, Thomas leaped out of the saddle, pulling her into his arms, swinging her around, kissing her on the lips. The people cheered, as they watched his men stand in their stirrups shouting, "Hooray! Hooray!"

Greater Love Hath No Man

Chapter twenty-seven

Some that had never visited Carter Town before were astonished at all the food and drink that was on hand in the middle of the most inflationary time of history.

"Where are all these people coming from?" Caroline asked Thomas, as they strolled by the front of the barn.

Pointing, Thomas asked, "Did you say Sarah helped you make that flag?"

"Yes. Rosemary gave us a few ideas too," she replied.

"That's why you see all these people here. They're hungry," Thomas answered.

Caroline never understood the depth of Thomas' remark. "Oh, Thomas, they didn't even know about that silly old flag, until now," she said, as they continued to move through the crowd. At times they would stop to talk to different families.

Thomas' three men stood at the corral fence with several miners, pulling the cork. Thomas walked up to them, as one of his men passed the jug to another.

Thomas said, "I'll be back in a minute. There's something I need to see about." Knowing the need of some one to watch for surprise attacks, he sent each man to post lookouts at three separate entrances.

Dan watched as the three men rode out. He waited for the right opportunity and then walked to Thomas. "I need to speak to you a minute," he said quietly.

"What about?" Thomas asked worriedly.

"Simmons is in the settlement and probably on his way here by now," Dan said.

Thomas listened, staring at the ground. "Who else knows about this?" He asked.

"Well, you might ought to know that the Davenports are camped at the west end of town near John Carter's place."

"Have they been informed?" Thomas asked.

"Informed and spoiling for a fight."

"How many has the old man got with him?"

"The entire clan. Even some of the women and kids are toting."

"Dang it! That's all we need now in the midst of all these people. A blood bath!"

"A couple of other things you might want to know, too. Simmons has Henry," Dan said.

"Where did you get your information?"

"John Carter," Dan answered. Thomas bit his lip and started to walk back toward Caroline. Dan caught him by the arm. "Wait. Before you go, there's something else," Dan whispered. "Major, you should be made aware that Simmons has sworn to hang you and your brother."

"Yeah," snickered Thomas. "and he also swore to hang John Carter's boys alongside me. I didn't know he added Henry to his list. The fool must have needed a substitute for Eli. Where's John Carter?" he asked.

"Who knows? Chadwick said he didn't come home last night," Dan answered.

"Who else knows about this besides you and John?" Thomas asked.

"No one but Chad and that kid from Arkansas," Dan answered.

Pausing for a few seconds, Thomas remarked, "Chadwick is good in a fight. This kid; can he be trusted?"

"He's your brother's friend," Dan answered.

The music started playing and several groups formed and began dancing the round dance, while others helped themselves to the food and drink.

Dan searched the crowd for Rosemary, as Thomas walked to Caroline, and side-by-side they strolled among the people. Stopping at the punch bowl, they began a conversation with one of the local farmers. Other farmers were starting to hover around, asking questions about the war. One of Thomas' men walked in and beckoned him.

"Please excuse me," he said.

"I think you need to come with me, Major. There's a fellow in front of the doctor's house wanting to speak with you. Said he had a message from that Yankee Major."

Halfway up the hill, in front of the house, Simmons' informant sat patiently, waiting for Thomas.

Dan watched them as they left. Then he motioned for Arkie and Chadwick, and the three followed. When

Thomas walked up to the man, he greeted him saying, "Major Thomas Watkins, at your service, sir."

"You're not a Major in any army I recognize," the horseman snarled. "Watkins, you and your men have one hour to lay down your arms and surrender, or we're coming in after you."

"Apparently, sir, your Major fails to understand how many people are here," Thomas said dryly.

"Now, Watkins, you know my Major couldn't care less how many are here. I take you to be a practical man. Give it up, Watkins. Besides, the vast majority of these people are northern loyalists, and I'm sure they wouldn't mind seeing their enemies removed."

"Sir, your friend the Major again fails to understand that I'm not an enemy to any Southerner or his property. We have merely tried to defend all Virginians from northern aggression. These people are Virginians, sir. Whether it's west; east; north; or south, we are Virginians, and Virginians refuse to be roughshod and plowed under by ambitious military officers," Thomas argued.

"Time is slipping away, Watkins," the informer growled.

"Then sir, take this message to your Major. The man he holds prisoner is my brother. I can assure you that he's not a solider of any army, and if he's harmed in any manner, you'll come to know how Virginians don't take kindly to hanging innocent people," Thomas continued.

The informant refused to speak another word and turned his horse to ride away. "Before you go, sir, may I ask which way you rode in here?"

"The same way I'm going back," he shouted.

Reaching for his Arkansas toothpick, Arkie said, "Hey mister, what makes you think you're gonna get back down that hill?"

"Watkins, I'll shoot that pup! Better call him off."

"Arkansas! Put that thing away," Thomas ordered. "You go tell your Major Simmons, I'll think on his offer."

The men watched as the man rode down the hill. "You just gonna let him ride out like that?" Chadwick asked.

"Just like that," Thomas answered. When Thomas walked back toward the party, he noticed Dan was gone. "Where's Holland?" he asked Chadwick.

"Davenports, I suppose. You don't think we're gonna let them take us down without firing a shot do you?"

"I said I would think on his offer, and the Davenports are not in my thoughts," Thomas said.

"Well sir, what are we gonna do? It's sure not in my plans to surrender," Chadwick remarked.

"Nor in mine, Private Carter, but a fight in the midst of all these people is definitely not the answer," Thomas said. "Arkansas, get your horse, and try to catch up with Holland and bring him back here if you can, but whatever you do, don't let the Davenports know about this."

Some of the people who were listening spread the news like wild fire.

Caroline trembled as she watched Thomas approach her. There would be no words. Looking deep into her eyes he kissed her on the forehead. Many times she had seen that certain look that encouraged her of his safe return, but this time it was different. He squeezed her hand, and then he slowly walked to his men.

The music continued and people danced, suspecting nothing. With a deep sadness, she walked to where Rosemary stood. Reaching for her hand, she began weeping. Rosemary embraced her. "Thomas is leaving, isn't he?" she asked.

A miner's wife watched as Rosemary comforted Caroline. "Is her man riding out with that Rebel officer?" she asked.

Greater Love Hath No Man

"That Rebel officer *is* her man," Rosemary said angrily.

"I'm so sorry. My husband overheard them fellows talking. Looks like he's gonna do it," she said, sadly.

"Do what?" Rosemary asked anxiously.

"They's wanting her man to surrender, so they can hang him," she replied.

When Caroline heard this, she pulled away from Rosemary and ran to the house. She reached her father's study. Without knocking, she barged in and found the room empty. Bonner watched as she ran down the hall, shouting, "Poppa! Poppa!"

"Miss Caroline, what's ailing you child?" Bonner asked.

"Yankees!" she cried. "I've got to find Poppa! Where's Poppa?"

"Your poppa and his brother is gone down there to dem Davenports. One of dem Davenport ladies done having herself a baby," Bonner said.

"It don't take two doctors to help a woman have a baby. Hitch me something to ride," Caroline ordered.

Trotting out the back door, Bonner called back, "Yes, ma'am."

Running to the barn, he almost knocked Rosemary down. "Pardon, Miss Rosemary. Miss Caroline is in a powerful hurry about something."

"Are you going to hitch up the buggy?" she asked.

"Yes, ma'am," he replied.

"Bring it around front, and hurry," she ordered.

Mumbling every step of the way, Bonner said, "White folks. Dey sho' is hard to understand. Always in a hurry bout sumpin."

Leaving Caroline to wait on Bonner, Rosemary walked to her room. She rummaged through her luggage and found a sealed envelope. She put it down in her blouse.

As she walked down the hall, she met Henry's wife, Mildred. "Have you seen the girls?" Mildred asked.

Not wanting her to know anything, she said, "The last I saw of them, they were playing near those miners' wagons with some other girls." Mildred thanked her and walked back down the hall, suspecting nothing.

Bonner stopped the buggy and got out, handing Caroline the whip. The two women got in, and like a flash they were off, with Caroline whipping the horse to a fast run.

"Slow down, Caroline," Rosemary ordered. "you're going to get us all killed, including the horse," she shouted.

Thomas and Chadwick sat on their horses near the charred remains of Lancaster's general store. Thomas knew when the two women drove up, that they had found out. Caroline stopped the buggy near the two horsemen and sat quietly staring. Rosemary got out and walked around. Thomas dismounted and walked to Caroline.

"Why did you come?" he asked. "This is no place for you. Go back to the party. I'll be along in a little while."

She continued to look into his eyes, quietly, while dust from the Federal column could be seen in a distance.

Her refusal to speak caused Thomas to pat the back of her hand and walk away. He mounted his horse and slowly started back to the big oak. He had tried sending Chadwick away as he had Arkie and Dan, but Chadwick refused to go.

Rosemary walked back to the buggy and sat down. "You should have at least said something to him," she whispered.

Caroline remained silent, staring into space. Rosemary took the envelope from her bosom and opened it. When she finished reading it, she slowly folded the paper and placed it back.

Greater Love Hath No Man

The sound of explosions from the Smithy's fireworks could be heard near the Glass' home. "Nothing like a good Fourth of July celebration, now is there?" smiled Chadwick.

Chapter twenty-eight

The Federal column raised a lot of dust as they rode through Carter Town. People that were camped near the roads wore handkerchiefs across their faces, trying to breath. Simmons and his informant rode side-by-side, in front of the column. Directly behind them, Henry rode his big gray, accompanied by a young sergeant.

Simmons raised his arm, giving the command to stop, as he approached Thomas. When the dust settled, Simmons ordered the sergeant to bring Henry to the front of the column. Thomas watched every move. Simmons ordered his men to form a circle, surrounding the entire area.

Greater Love Hath No Man

Caroline and Rosemary watched as they closed in the gap directly behind them. A lump formed in Chadwick's throat. The Glass brothers drove up in the surrey hoping to see what was happening.

Thomas watched as Rosemary ran to her father.

The doctor got out, and with Rosemary following, walked toward Simmons, pushing aside two Union horsemen. "What's the meaning of this?" he shouted at Simmons.

"Who are you, and what concern is this to you?"

"My name is Doctor Charles Glass, from Mineral Wells and I demand to know by what authority do you hang a Union solider?"

"Sir, I'm not hanging a Union solider, but I'm hanging a spy and two Confederate troublemakers."

Walking to Henry, the doctor said, "Sir, this man is a union soldier, and I have proof of it."

When the doctor said those words, the Baker boy broke rank and rode to where they were, with the sergeant following close behind shouting, "Soldier, get back in rank."

Rosemary handed her father the written agreement that the Bakers had signed. "Sir, they're right," shouted the young man. "I'm serving in Mr. Watkins' place under the conscription law."

Simmons read the paper and stood in his stirrups, to rest his back. "What is your name trooper?" he asked.

"Baker, sir. Private Baker."

"Well Private, why haven't you let me know this before now?" Simmons asked.

"I have tried, sir, several times, but the sergeant refused to let me see you," he said.

"Get back to your position, trooper," ordered the commander. "Sergeant, release the prisoner, but keep him here. I want him to watch when we hang these Rebels."

Dr. Glass again pleaded with Simmons to reconsider his decision about Thomas and Chadwick. "Doctor, your proof convinced me that my prisoner was innocent. However, Doctor, may I remind you, sir, that this is war and those two Rebels are our enemies."

"Yours, maybe sir, but definitely not mine or the state of West Virginia," Dr. Glass answered.

"Well, nevertheless, Doctor, I will do as I please in this matter," Simmons stated.

When Caroline heard those words, she leaped from the buggy and running, she shouted, "No! No! You can't do this!"

Simmons shouted to another trooper, "Seize her!"

When the trooper broke rank to pick her up, and before Thomas could reach for his pistol, Simmons fell from his horse with a bullet in the back of his head, knocking him to the ground. With arms drawn, every trooper stood in their stirrups, trying to see where the shot came from.

Echoes from the sound of the smithy's fireworks continued in the distance. They wondered whether they'd ever know who fired the fatal shot that killed Simmons, or which direction it came from that day, but it was certain that Carter Town wouldn't shed a tear.

A young militia officer ordered a detail to carry Simmons' body away. Stopping his mount in front of Thomas and Caroline, he said, "Sir, it's obvious that this was a personal matter. The state of West Virginia has no quarrel with you or any of your family."

Looking around and seeing hundreds of people standing near, Thomas pointed to them, saying, "Sir, this is my family."

The officer sat erect in his saddle and saluted Thomas. "Sir, I offer my apologies for the behavior of my former commander, but as long as you and your men wear those uniforms, you are an enemy to these United States of

America. However, if you and your men lay your weapons aside and return to your families, I will assure you that as long as I am in command of this troop, we will not interfere in your lives, again."

Thomas removed his side arm and handed it to Caroline while the others did the same. "What you have here is the way it should be everywhere." With that, the union officer turned and led his soldiers away.

The people returned to the Glass' barn and found the women and children huddled together, waiting for the worst. When they saw their men folk coming, they ran to greet them.

Leading the crowd was Mildred and her daughters, as they ran to Henry. He saw them coming and ran to meet them. They collided and the four rolled on the ground, laughing and crying, hugging and everyone trying to talk at the same time.

When the crowd had settled a little so that Doctor Glass could be heard, he shouted, "Folks, come inside. I have some news for all of you."

Just as the people gathered and settled, John Carter, Dan Holland, and Arkie came riding into the yard.

"Looks like there's a party goin' on," said Dan.

Arkie looked at him as though he was dense and replied, "They is, you idjit! We been working on it three days now!"

John looked at the sky and said, "Lord, are these two the only millstones you could find to tie around my neck?" The three friends entered the barn, laughing.

The crowd in the huge barn became quiet as Dr. Glass approached the podium. He perched his glasses on the end of his nose and shuffled paper as he cleared his throat.

"Citizens of Carter Town," he began, "visitors, friends and neighbors: welcome." The crowd cheered, causing the doctor some embarrassment. "Please!" he said, as he waved for quiet.

"We have gathered here today in a celebration of life and love. I stand here, looking into the faces of those who have given so much during this war, which none of us wanted and that some of us have tried to avoid. Yet, our fellow countrymen have marched across our homes and farms, our communities and our settlements, killing and destroying everything in their path. Those of us who have fought, have done so in defense of our homes and families and those of our neighbors.

"As I think of those brave souls, I am reminded of the Davenports, who fought bravely and lost so many family members. We have buried the same children whom I delivered. Our children. Our husbands and our brothers have lost their lives for a cause that has no affect on us. We are not slave owners! We are mountain people, free and independent.

"John Carter has given a son to this war, and the one who left here as a boy has returned as a man, forever changed." Doctor Glass paused a moment to wipe his eyes.

"Look around you for the faces that are missing from our midst. Our good neighbor Henry Watkins who lost his home and barns to marauding villains in uniforms. They destroyed his livestock for no reason and treated him as a prisoner of war, while his family was left to fend for themselves, and in spite of everything, you gathered lumber and supplies, rebuilt what was destroyed and helped them by sharing the stock you had.

"His brother, Thomas, with his ragtag volunteers leading the soldiers away from us, helped save so many lives here. Now, they are here, again, reunited as family, as I am with my brother.

"I could go on with the endless list of selfless acts of you folks and even those of my own daughter and my niece. There is no way to thank those who have given the ultimate sacrifice, but in a simple way I will borrow the words of one greater than all of us as I read from the gospel of St. John, 15:13: greater love hath no man than this, that a man lay down his life for his friends."

He closed his book and removed his glasses. The crowd stood quietly, waiting for Doctor Glass to continue.

"Now let us celebrate our rebirth as a state, our rebirth as a community, and a rebirth of friends and family as our heroes return home. Let us celebrate life with singing and dancing. To us, in the mountains of the great state of West Virginia, at least, this war is over and may we never forget that mountaineers are always free."

Thomas loved every word that was being said, and for a few minutes he hid his true feelings. He looked around and watched as everyone seemed to be having a good time but deep down inside he knew there would be more Simmons.

While the town's people were having a moment to remember, little did they know that not far away, in the state of Pennsylvania, in a little town named Gettysburg, the southern cause had fought harder than ever for its existence and now while they were drinking and eating, General Robert E. Lee was leading his battered army southward after leaving thousands of dead and wounded that created the name, "High Water Mark."

Charles Dale & Ross Wood

About the Authors

Charles Dale has always loved history, especially the period of the Great Civil War. After years of research and digging through archives, visiting the different battlefields and speaking personally with descendants of those who fought in this war, Mr. Dale has captured the true spirit of the people of early America.

He has succeeded in putting onto paper, the emotions of a people who really didn't want a war and simply wanted to be left alone. This story will cause you to laugh, to cry and to celebrate with the people as you go with them to overcome the hardships they faced in those tragic days.

Co-authored by his lifelong friend, Ross Wood, an accomplished writer and former newspaper publisher, these two gentlemen take you to the heart of the people of West Virginia, The Mountaineers. Brave people who refused to relinquish their freedom or their principles for a political cause. They have written a book that when you finish the last page, you have a tear in your eye and your thoughts are, "What a wonderful story."

Charles lives in Northern Arkansas with his wife, and Ross resides in South Texas with his family.